Praise for *The R*

"A suspenseful ı
It's a gothic thriller, a medical horror story, a warning; most importantly, it's a great read!" **Johanna van Veen, author of *Blood on Her Tongue***

"*The Retreat* is both victim statement and witness testimony ... On the surface a story about a cult and its charismatic, sinister leader. It's also a moving portrayal of illness and the search for wellness ... and how in that quest, friendship and love can sometimes lose their way." **Tim Lebbon, author of *Secret Lives of the Dead***

"Eerie and unsettling, *The Retreat* draws you in, weaving a sense of uncertainty as it blurs the lines between fiction and reality. A commentary on the cultish possibilities of wellness culture ... I took one bite of this book and couldn't stop until I'd devoured it all." **Angie Spoto, author of *The Bone Diver***

"A deliciously dark, compelling story of desperation and exploitation that leaves the reader with a chill on the spine. An addictive book!" **Elizabeth Lee, author of *Cunning Women***

"A chilling tale of the terrors and tragedies involved in a shady healing cult, led by a charismatic and manipulative individual who preys on the lonely, the desperate and the lost ... Gemma Fairclough's unnerving narrative is stripped of melodrama and all the more horrific as a result." **Rosie Garland, author of *The Fates***

Praise for *Bear Season*:

"Bloody hell! *Bear Season* is terrific. A supremely confident blend of found-footage, true crime, and dark fairy tales that I found utterly impossible to put down. Fairclough's debut refuses easy answers and categorisation ... Simply addictive." **Ally Wilkes, author of *All the White Spaces***

"Mystery and longing intertwine seductively in this compelling exploration of three women's minds ... where desire, grief and fear take on wilder forms, and human nature might blur with animal instinct. *Bear Season* asks: what does each of us conceal, under our pelts?" **Zoe Gilbert, author of *Folk* an *Mischief Acts***

"A deft, thoughtful, unique gem of a book. Crafted with care, skill and sensitivity, it weaves together tension, mystery, ambiguity and obsession, questioning the stories we live and tell ... Innovative, atmospheric and unsettling." **Jane Claire Bradley, author of *Dear Neighbour***

The Retreat

Gemma Fairclough

Wild Hunt Books

The Retreat
First published in 2025 by Wild Hunt Books
wildhuntbooks.co.uk

A CIP catalogue record for this title is available from the British Library

Paperback: 978-1-0685631-2-6
Ebook: 978-1-0685631-3-3

Cover Design by Luísa Dias
Edited by Ariell Cacciola
Typeset by Wild Hunt Books

The Northern Weird Project is a registered trademark of Wild Hunt Books

THE RETREAT

Richard Blackley is a writer and retired academic originally from Salford, Greater Manchester. Working for nearly thirty years in the field of public health, his articles have been published in numerous peer-reviewed journals. Alongside his academic career, Blackley is a passionate fell-walker and wrote a popular blog on his rambling exploits; in his later years, he became a freedom-to-roam activist, contributing letters on the topic to *The Guardian*. Upon retiring, he relocated to Cumbria with his family and set to work on his memoirs, originally conceived as a collection of pieces about his rambles in the Lake District. However, he soon became embroiled in another project entirely, to which he dedicated himself until he became incapacitated due to illness. What follows is the manuscript of this project, entitled *The Retreat*.

Hartman Retreat Centre (Blundale Hall)
Blundale
Cumbria
CA11 0NX
1st May 1992

Dear Mum and Dad,

I am sorry for my behaviour over the past few months and if I gave you a scare. The good news is you can stop worrying. I'm doing much better now.

Claire's mum probably told you already, but I handed in my notice a few weeks ago. Nursing isn't for me. This might seem sudden to you, but for me it's been a long time coming. It was making me more ill – the long hours, relentless pressure, all that suffering and death.

I thought I had no other choice until I read *Toxic People* – have you heard of it? This book saved me. It helped me understand what was wrong with me, modern medicine, and society in general. I was complicit in a broken system, and the first step to making the world a better place was to change what I could in my own life.

You'll have noticed the different address. After reading *Toxic People*, I found out the author runs a retreat in the Lake District. It sounded perfect. I needed time away to process things and not get caught up in the same old unhealthy patterns. The house is straight out of a Jane Austen novel. It's got a grand staircase and high ceilings and chandeliers. You'd love it, Mum. It's next to a mountain, and there are woods and a lake and fields full of flowers. I've taken some pictures (not that they do it justice). Only there's nowhere to get them developed around here! I love how quiet and peaceful it is.

They say you should never meet your heroes, but in this case, I'm glad I did. Charles Hartman is one of the kindest people I've ever met. I was nervous when I arrived, but he's so welcoming and made me feel right at home. The other residents are friendly, too. People of all ages and different walks of life, yet we're all likeminded – all big fans of Charles! We do group walks, yoga, and loads of other activities, but we also live as a community. We make and eat our meals together. You won't believe it, Mum, but I'm learning how to cook! And not just stuff out of a packet. We make everything from scratch, even bread, and we grow and forage the ingredients onsite. My fingers are turning green from all the wild garlic.

I'm not sure when I'm coming back yet. My pains have completely stopped since I arrived. I feel better than ever! Charles says I can stay as long as I want and offered me a discount. I know I'll need to come home soon, get a new job and so on. Still, I'm happy where I am, for now. I'm using some of my savings for my room and board, but I'll still have enough to invest in my future and retrain in something else when I get back.

Anyway, I hope this reassures you both. Is everyone keeping well?

Lots of love,

Julie

xxx

28th September 1992

Dear Mum and Dad,

Thanks for the birthday card, and sorry for not replying to your letters sooner. I've hardly had a moment to myself, with the summer harvest and prep for winter. I know it might seem early to be thinking about winter, but when you don't get your food from a supermarket, there's a lot to plan ahead of the seasons changing!

I should have said – there's no telephone at the house, hence why it's not in the Yellow Pages. Sorry for the confusion. For now, it's best if we stick to letters, please. I can't come back for a visit yet, but maybe Christmas could work.

Of course they're feeding me ... if anything, I'm eating better than you! Nothing but homemade food made with organic ingredients produced onsite. No pesticides, additives, or nasty chemicals of any kind. I'm being well looked after – please stop worrying!!! – but I'm also working hard and learning lots. The work is much more satisfying than nursing (which I don't miss AT ALL). Charles says the straightforward, hard graft of manual labour returns us to a simpler way of living, which helps us attune to our spiritual needs. Did you read the book yet? (Mum – hope you had a nice birthday!)

I'm not quite ready to come back. My health's improved loads, but I want to make sure I'm totally better. I hope you'll understand and respect my decision.

That's lovely news about Richard and Jen, although it's weird thinking of him being a dad! Can you imagine him trying to talk to a baby?! Reprimanding its poor diction. Thanks for letting me know the date of the wedding – I'm hoping I can make it.

Hope you're all okay.

Love,

Julie

xxx

15th January 1993

Dear Mum and Dad,

Happy New Year. Sorry I wasn't able to make it for Christmas, but you shouldn't have gone over the top, sending all that stuff. We had to throw the hamper away – as I've told you, we don't consume anything produced offsite that might be toxic. There was no need to send on cards from the entire family. Please don't do that again. Otherwise, Charles might have to ban us from sending or receiving post. It's disrupting our healing. He only agreed to me writing this letter because I promised I'd convince you to show more restraint.

Charles and I have gotten very close. Even though there are plenty of other women here, including younger and thinner and prettier ones, Charles says I'm special. He praises me for the progress I've made, although I've still got a way to go. I can't give up now. You're always saying you hope I'll meet someone nice to spend my life with. I really feel I've found the right person.

I hope you're all OK, but please wait at least three weeks before sending another letter.

Love,

Julie

x

31st January 1993

Mum and Dad,

I'm so angry with you I can barely write. But I have to make you understand.

Turning up at the house without any notice was unacceptable. Of course Karma and Noah wouldn't let you in, especially with you both shouting and going on. I heard Dad threatening to call the police, which made no sense – I'm not here against my will. I'm a grown woman. I've asked you to respect my decisions but you won't.

This will be my last letter. Charles is banning post, thanks to what you did. He says it was a bad idea allowing it in the first place, since it distracts us from our healing, which is what we came here to do. You seem to have forgotten how unwell I was before. Don't you want me to be healthy?

You're both caught up in toxic ways of thinking – all that pollution and bad food is rotting your brains. So much so you couldn't understand a word of Charles's book. He's really upset with me because of all this. He says I'm too attached to my old life. I have to break off with it if I'm ever going to heal.

Please do not write to me again. Charles is paying for a new secure fence and gate around the grounds, so there's no point attempting another visit either.

Julie

4th January 1994

Dear Mum,

I'm back at Claire's at the moment (as I'm sure you're now aware – I know Claire's mum went round to see you). It's only temporary while I look for work and a flat. I didn't want to bother you and Dad until I'd got myself sorted. I've not been well recently, hence why I've not called or written sooner.

If it's okay, I'll phone on Saturday at 7 o'clock.

Love,

Julie

Recollections

My sister, Julie Blackley, was found dead on the thirtieth of January 1994. She was thirty years old. Her friend, Claire, with whom she was living at the time, came home from work and discovered the body. The coroner recorded the cause of death as asphyxia due to hanging with a verdict of suicide. Her death was not treated as suspicious.

The last time I saw Julie was Christmas, 1991.

This was back when Jen and I still hadn't broken tradition of spending the holiday with our respective families rather than each other. Although we lived together ('Living in sin,' Mum liked to say, smirking, with only a hint of genuine disapproval), we were as yet unmarried, in part because we rejected marriage as a regressive institution and the relic of a bygone era, and also because we were immersed in our burgeoning academic careers as much as each other. This led my parents to believe I was living in a prolonged adolescence at the age of thirty-seven. Shortly after my arrival on Christmas Eve, Dad wondered aloud when I might get myself a 'proper job', his adage whenever I returned home. I attempted to explain I was coming to the end of a fixed-term research position while seeking a permanent post combining research and teaching. Alas, my defence fell on deaf ears. The inner workings of academia meant little to my parents, who'd never been to university. Though they were proud of my achievements in a general sense. On the living room wall, Mum had hung my three graduation photos along with those of my younger siblings, all except Julie.

My married siblings were spared from festivities with our parents. Those of us without such claims to legitimate adulthood were expected to stay overnight on Christmas Eve, join Mum and Dad at Mass in the morning (atheism was no excuse not to attend, apparently), and then, from two o'clock in the afternoon, sit at the overfilled dining table and eat until we all had acid reflux.

I was frustrated, having waited all day to telephone Jen. Only Mum had found something else for me to do at every opportunity. What I'd looked forward to most was seeing Julie, exchanging smirks over the mountains of food when one of our parents said something ridiculous. But all through dinner she had been avoiding my eye and giving cursory responses to my questions about her job at the nursing home, which I thought I'd posed sufficiently neutrally.

While Mum ignited and served the Christmas pudding, my brother, Luke, who'd studied Biology, told us about the conservation project he was managing down in Dartmoor. Julie listened intently as he described the driest details of his work; meanwhile, I drained my fourth glass of red wine. I don't remember exactly what I said – something flippant about how Julie could have been a scientist herself by now, finding a cure for cancer, but instead she was too busy wiping arses – but I can't forget her reaction. She became hysterical. She jumped to her feet and screamed she was sick of being criticised. Pointing at me, she shouted, 'You don't know what's best for me. You don't even know me. Just stay out of my life.' She ran upstairs and we all flinched as her bedroom door slammed shut.

'Oh, Richard, why'd you have to upset her,' Mum said, shaking her head.

'It was only a joke,' I said, defensively.

Dad pulled off his pink paper crown and muttered about Julie being too sensitive. This turned into a whispered instalment of the long-standing, recurring topic of conversation between my parents and siblings, neighbours, and whoever else would listen: *What's Wrong With Julie.*

The problems began in her final year of primary school. Her teachers pronounced her gifted, miles ahead of her peers in any subject when she gave her full attention. Only, she had difficulty concentrating. No matter, we thought, this was only a phase. There was no question she would go to university, a fate preordained for all my younger siblings after I began my degree, the first to do so in my family.

Mum wanted all her children to succeed. She'd left school without qualifications, married young, and had children. While her husband went out to work, she stayed home, a good Catholic wife; that had been the way of things. But times had changed, and women might 'have it all' if they worked hard enough. So, it was concerning when Julie, a ten-year-old girl with the luxury of having everything ahead of her, complained of nausea that prevented her from completing her homework, headaches that made her fail tests, abdominal cramps that kept her home from school.

Mum took Julie to the family GP. He found no fault with Julie other than she was growing up. Her symptoms were nothing more than the routine discomfort all women should expect at 'that time of the month'.

Despite having this explained to her, and the regular dispensation of paracetamol, Julie continued crying off school because of aches and pains.

Dad did not know what to make of this development of Julie's. He had trouble accepting sick days from any of us, himself having never missed school or work. Matters of women's health were especially mystifying, and he turned deaf whenever Mum spoke of Julie having 'women's troubles'. If the discussion persisted, he'd flee the room for some undefined purpose elsewhere.

I fought against my own shame about this topic to ask Mum what exactly was making Julie ill. She would only discuss the matter euphemistically, with great deal of sighing and headshaking. From the limited information I could gather, there was nothing physically wrong with Julie. She just didn't want to apply herself.

I hadn't been spending as much time with Julie –
I'd been down in London, studying – but I couldn't
believe she'd become lazy. Although there were ten years
between us, we'd always been close while I lived at
home. I used to check over her homework (invariably
flawless) and take her to the library on weekends, where
she skipped past the children's section in favour of
'the big books'. On rainy Sunday afternoons, we'd play
chess and discuss human anatomy, dinosaurs, atoms,
the universe. She'd knock on my bedroom door to ask
if she could listen to my records with me – my brilliant sister, who danced around my room when I put
on Black Sabbath's 'Paranoid'. Surely something worse
than menstrual pain was causing this extremely intelligent girl to retreat from school and hole up in her
bedroom with the curtains drawn.

Psychiatry has never been my favourite branch of
medicine – it's rather too woolly and metaphysical
for my liking – yet I proffered Julie's illness may have
a mental basis as opposed to a physical one. Mum
wouldn't accept this idea; as far as she was concerned,
our parochial doctor's diagnosis was gospel. I knew I'd
have no chance convincing Dad, who was even more
dismissive of mental illness than 'coughs and sniffles'.
They decided to send Julie to a convent school, where
minimal distractions, firm discipline, and a stronger
sense of Catholic duty might nip her indolence in the
bud.

The first time Julie went, as Dad put it, 'off the rails',
Mum rang and filled me in on the incident at school:

Julie rudely answering back to the Sister presiding over her class, who had denied her permission to go to the toilet; then, when the Sister ordered Julie to stay behind for detention during break time, Julie screamed as though possessed, frightening the other girls.

Mum begged me to have a word with her. 'She might listen to you.'

At grammar school, I'd encountered my own share of sadistic teachers, never mind despotic nuns. They hadn't taken kindly to being corrected by a precocious teenage boy; my palms still winced in memory of the cane.

'Just get through your O-levels and A-levels, then you can leave home and go to university, and be whoever you want to be,' I told Julie. Solid advice from my own experience.

In spite of my efforts to guide her, however, the distance between us grew during her teens. She was evasive when I asked about her plans for the future, which A-level subjects she wanted to take. She draped herself in black leather and listened to punk, which I do not consider music. I assumed she'd grow out of it.

Mum and Dad were continually at the end of their tether with her. When she got sacked from her Saturday job for repeated absence, Dad was devastated: no Blackley had ever been sacked before – they'd resigned, been made redundant, yes, but never sacked. I told him he was overreacting and surely incorrect. Similarly, I tried to temper Mum's histrionics when Julie ran away to live at Claire's house. Since primary school, Julie had been best friends with Claire: a distinctly average but good-natured, down-to-earth girl – not some malign influence stealing Julie away, as Mum had suddenly decided. I suggested a change of environment might even be good for Julie.

How wrong I was.

What truly upset me was her dropping out of school. After that, I tended to keep out of things, listening to Mum's telephone updates with stoical detachment. Julie – the brightest girl in her class – scraped only a couple of O-levels. Menial jobs followed: she worked as an office cleaner; a croupier; a trader on a market stall, selling incense sticks and 'healing crystals' to dreadlocked dimwits. There was a string of ne'er-do-well boyfriends, including a biker and a hippie, then a surprising, sudden marriage to accountant, which only lasted a few years, dashing Mum's hopes of her starting a family.

Then Mum told me Julie was attending night school. It seemed liked the start of her turning her life around, achieving her full potential, until I learned she was training to be a nurse: a career that made no sense for a woman with her gifts, or so I believed then.

My parents, at least, were satisfied. Nursing was a respectable profession with a decent salary and job security. Lines of communication with Julie reopened. She came home for visits, even stayed over at Christmas. For a while, we all played Happy Families, until Christmas, 1991.

In the dark, damp weeks of January and February 1992, Mum phoned me with worsening reports on Julie.

'She's not been turning up for work.' The worry in Mum's voice was as familiar and etched into my memory as Julie's name.

She'd heard about it from Jackie, Claire's mum. According to Jackie via Claire, Julie had been off sick, citing stress and abdominal pain. She didn't want to come out for a drink anymore; she stayed home alone, reading self-help books. Julie refused to talk about it. Mum didn't know what to do.

'Do you think you could talk to her?' she asked.

'After what happened at Christmas? I don't think so.' I laughed, even though I wasn't the least bit amused. What Julie had said to me still stung.

'She could lose her job!'

'She'll get another one. They always need more nurses, don't they? Anyway, I don't see what we can do about it. Julie doesn't want us interfering.'

The next update I recall was in the spring, when Mum told me Julie had gone to a retreat in Cumbria. She was very taken with the man who ran the place. I scoffed at how someone as intelligent as Julie could be so silly.

Mum sounded more hopeful. 'She seems to be doing much better. And this bloke's done well for himself, from the sounds of things. Julie says he writes books.'

Julie's relationship record gave me no reason to share Mum's positive outlook.

In the months that followed, Mum fretted about not hearing from Julie. When she finally did, it turned out Julie had no plans to return. I told Mum to let Julie get on with it; at my lowest ebb, I may have said Julie was being selfish as always. I was tired of having the same conversation over and over. Also, I had preoccupations of my own: in June, Jen found out she was pregnant, and we'd decided to get married ahead of the baby arriving. I'd also started a new role as Lecturer in Public Health at the University of East London. I was spread thin; I had no time to think of Julie's latest nonsense.

Jen and I married that October. We held the wedding back up North, and the whole family attended apart from Julie. I kept looking for her face in the church and, afterwards, in the function room, where we had a buffet and a DJ – extraordinary circumstances given mine and Jen's once-lofty ideals – and it was only as people were starting to leave that I understood Julie would not be coming.

For the first time in my life, I was granted a reprieve from spending Christmas with my parents, being married with a baby on the way. Jen and I had finally left the crumbling Hackney flat we'd resided in since the late seventies and moved into a Woodford terrace. Strangely, I missed the certainty of previous years' proceedings. Nothing would ever be the same. On Christmas Eve, while Jen and I were stringing tinsel around light fittings in a vain attempt to summon holiday spirit, the phone rang.

'Julie said she might come for Christmas,' Mum said, her voice quiet and strained down the line, 'but she hasn't arrived yet. We haven't heard from her since September.'

'Hasn't even sent a Christmas card!' Dad called from elsewhere in the room.

'Well, what did you expect? She didn't even come to my wedding,' I said, surprised to find my voice catching. I'd always thought it was ridiculous to make a big deal out of weddings, but Julie's absence from mine hurt more than I'd cared to admit.

A couple of weeks before Olivia was born, at the end of January, Mum phoned again, upset and agitated. I had to ask her to slow down and repeat herself.

She said she and Dad had gone up to Cumbria to visit Julie and 'have it out with her', but 'those odd people' wouldn't let them in the house.

'We didn't see Julie. I don't know if she knew we were there. Oh, they were so rude to us, Richard.'

Dad grumbled in the background. 'Looked like scruffy gits, the lot of them!'

After this incident, Mum and Dad stopped volunteering information about Julie, and it got to the point when I had to ask them for updates. Mum kept saying she didn't feel like talking about it until Dad entreated me to stop asking; apparently, Julie had cut contact with them. Holding Olivia as she slept, swaddled in her yellow blanket (Jen resolved our daughter would not wear pink unless she told us she wanted to), a bubble of spit on her tiny wet lips, I wondered if my daughter would ever be capable of causing this much distress to her parents. However, my concerns about Julie were quickly overshadowed by the daily pressures of work and home life. I was determined to keep my promise to Jen to do my fair share of housework and childcare, and not go the way of our fathers and grandfathers and so many men before me.

By Christmas, 1993, Julie remained absent from the family gathering, but there was news. Jackie had been round to see Mum and Dad, and she told them Julie was back in Salford, living at Claire's. My parents were furious they'd had to hear about Julie's return from her friend's mother. I asked Mum what had happened with the man in Cumbria: Charles Whatshisname? That appeared to be all over; there'd been no mention of him. According to Jackie, Claire said Julie kept going on about someone called Michael. So, perhaps she'd met someone new.

One evening in January, Mum called. She sounded shaken.

'I spoke to Julie on the phone just now, and she wasn't right. But she won't tell me what's going on. Just kept talking about this Michael. How Michael was angry with her. I don't know what she's supposed to have done. Could you go round to see her?'

'I wouldn't know what to say,' I said, 'We haven't spoken in years.' The thought of seeing Julie's face after all this time made me jittery.

'I'm worried about her, Richard.'

'Let me think on it.'

When that didn't reassure her, I added, 'I'll give her a call when I'm able. One day soon.'

That day never came.

It was painful to move on with life without Julie but move on we must.

A year, two years, a whole decade slipped by. My father died. My mother broke her hip. Olivia fell off her bike and broke her arm. Jen's career advanced faster than mine; she was appointed Head of the History department at Birmingham, and her book on medieval medicine achieved seminal status. She travelled abroad for academic conferences while I stayed home and took care of Olivia. Life's minutiae swallowed whole days, absorbing energy and attention, yet Julie was always there in the background, just beyond reach. Occasionally, she returned for an instant: in a familiar-sounding voice, or the smell of her perfume, or as a woman resembling her shape seen from afar – then she was gone again.

I dreamed of her often; in my dreams, she lived.

I experienced bouts of depression. I needed time off work, relying on Jen to juggle her demanding job and household responsibilities. She encouraged me to seek treatment. I tried medication and therapy, but what saved me was fell-walking.

Whenever I could, I visited national parks up and down the country. My firm favourite was the Lake District. My career, once so important to me, was eclipsed by mountains. When I wasn't out walking, I was keeping track of the weather forecast for favourable conditions, shopping for the best crampons and hiking poles and GPS device. I scaled down teaching and research to allow more time for walking, as well as blogging about the walks I'd completed. My blog got thousands of hits.

I discovered, to my chagrin, how much land in the Lake District is privately owned and closed off to the public. I got involved in freedom-to-roam campaigns, writing letters to newspapers and my MP about how the 2000 CRoW Act hadn't gone far enough; for instance, unrestricted access for walkers does not extend to woodland. I wrote a scathing blog post about a so-called 'wellness centre' in Blundale, owned by a company called Hart Health Group, which had created an access island that blocked all public routes to Lyfell Pike, effectively making it impossible to reach the mountain without breaking the law. Hart's solicitor wrote to me accusing me of libel and threatened legal action unless I took down this post. Amused by their exaggerated claim and blatant attempt at intimidation, which only fuelled my desire to keep writing and publishing criticisms of their corporate irresponsibility, I looked closer into the company. Its website said it was founded in 1979 by Charles Hartman.

Didn't Julie once live with a Charles?

I intended to ask Mum, but she would still not discuss Julie's death, nor the later years of Julie's life. Dad went to his grave without ever speaking of these matters with his surviving children. On numerous occasions over the years, I spoke of this with my sister, Sally – never within earshot of Mum, towards whom Sally had become fiercely protective.

'It's too much for her,' Sally explained. 'She blames herself for not doing enough for Julie.'

'But she must know there was more to it than that,' I said, thinking of the time I'd upset Julie at Christmas. 'It shouldn't feel shameful to talk about Julie. It's not healthy for Mum, for any of us, carrying around all this guilt.'

As it turned out, in 2006, it wasn't Mum's health I needed to worry about.

Jen found a lump in her breast and was diagnosed with Stage 3 breast cancer. My focus narrowed; my purview shrank. My sole priorities were supporting Jen as best as I could through her surgery and treatment alongside looking after Olivia, who was thirteen at the time. I had little time to spare for walking; I neglected my blog, on which previously I'd posted at least once a month. I panicked at receiving another email from the Hart Health Group's solicitor, prompting me to take down the offending post, where previously I'd have fought to keep it up. Defiance no longer seemed worthwhile; I didn't want any additional stress from a litigious company. Soon after, I took down the whole blog. I didn't have it in me anymore.

In 2008, Jen's cancer went into remission, and I could breathe again.

At the tail-end of 2009, my recession-spooked university was making cutbacks and offered a voluntary redundancy scheme with a generous lump sum payout. In my mid-fifties, being neither a faculty star nor a favourite among the students, I accepted. Academia no longer held my interest in any case; I was a cog in an institutional machine. After Olivia finished her A-levels, we sold our house in London and bought a cottage in Grange-over-Sands. It had always been our plan to move to Cumbria, and although Jen was nowhere near ready to retire (after her health scare, she'd dived back into work), she saw no reason to put off relocating. I adopted an ageing rescue dog, a beagle I named John Snow, to keep me company while Jen was working and Olivia was at university.

For Jen, the cottage was a haven from work; for me, it marked a new chapter, a space to embark on writing a book. I planned to repurpose a selection of my old blog posts for my memoir. I pitched it as Wainwright meets Robin Hood, taking the countryside back from private landowners and returning it to the masses. I even had a title – *Forgive Our Trespasses* – and a modest advance from a small independent publisher of socially-conscious creative non-fiction. Each day, I spent hours in my study working on the book, John Snow snorting as

he slept in a dog bed at my side. I'd take breaks from
writing to gaze out the window at Morecambe Bay and
watch waders and oystercatchers sink their beaks into
saltmarsh.

For a little while, life was calm and peaceful.

At the end of October 2012, just as another winter beckoned, Mum had a massive stroke. A couple of
weeks later, she passed away in hospital.

I drove down to Salford to join my siblings in clearing out my parents' house ahead of putting it on the
market. It was a lot of work; Mum and Dad had a
habit of holding onto items long after their use or val-
ue was lost. In their wardrobe were piles of shoeboxes
and ice cream tubs filled with decades-old coupons and
receipts, newspaper clippings, our old school reports.
In one shoebox, which Mum had enigmatically labelled
'Odds and Sods', I found a stack of envelopes tied together with red elastic band. I recognised Julie's handwriting instantly – a mature version of the looping,
precocious lettering that had once covered her school
exercise books. My hands shook as I pulled out and
unfolded the letters and read them one by one.

Sally found me kneeling on the carpet with the letters
spread around me. I'd combed through every detail. On
the fourth or fifth reading, I was struck by the return
address, which matched the address of the wellness centre that had threatened legal action against me several
years ago.

Why on earth had Mum and Dad never shown me
these letters? All my historic anger towards my reserved,

private parents resurged. It was obvious, reading these letters, that Julie had been lured into some sort of cult.

Unfathomably, my siblings did not agree.

'You're still looking for reasons why she killed herself,' said Sally.

'Something clearly wasn't right about this retreat,' I said, waving the stack of letters in their nonplussed faces. 'We should look into it.'

'Won't make any difference now, will it,' muttered Luke.

'If something happened to Julie at this place,' I pushed on, 'there'll be others.'

Sally sighed and shook her head. 'Julie was troubled.'

'It's been years, Rich,' said Luke. 'Can't you let it go?'

I would not 'let it go'. Something had happened to Julie, and Charles Hartman was responsible.

The Project

After Mum's funeral, grief infected me. My half-finished draft of *Forgive Our Trespasses* was abandoned; check-in emails from the publisher went unanswered. I stayed home, except to take John Snow for his constitutional; on the worst days, I couldn't even manage that. I couldn't think clearly. I kept making silly mistakes: misplacing my door keys and locking myself out; losing the car keys; mixing up names.

Jen persuaded me to go to the GP, who referred me to a memory clinic. After a run of tests and scans, I was called in for a consultation. Jen came with me.

'Have you been under any stress recently?' the consultant asked.

'Yes, my mother died. And ... some information about my sister came to light. She'd been in a cult. She died almost twenty years ago. Suicide.'

'I see. That must have been difficult.' The consultant glanced down at her notes. 'You have clinical depression?'

'I'd been on top of that until all this happened.'

'Doctor,' Jen cut in, 'is that what's causing the memory loss? Or something else?'

The unspoken word 'dementia' hovered in the room: a malevolent spirit.

Thankfully, the consultant exorcised it immediately. 'We found no signs of neurological disease. But we should take steps to manage the depression.'

She referred me to a psychiatrist, who prescribed medication and recommended counselling, as well as a bereavement support group. I'd tried all that in the past and it hadn't worked. However, it gave me an idea.

I did some Google searching and found a support group for survivors of cults. The group met one evening a month in Preston. Driving there would be easy enough. I sent a request to join the group via Facebook, and shortly after received an invitation to the next meeting. After weeks of lethargy, now I was bursting with energy, galvanised by the prospect of getting some answers.

I parked up outside the red-brick, single storey community hall and sat in my car, watching twenty or so adults, young and old, mostly women, file in through the red double doors.

Chairs were laid out in a circle in the middle of the hall. The group leader gave a general welcome, before asking for volunteers to share their experiences.

One by one, members of the group put themselves forward. Their stories were frustratingly vague, lacking detail. Some could barely remember what happened. I realise I'm being uncharitable here, but as someone seeking insight, I was disappointed. I'd felt the same way reading books and watching documentaries about cults; precise oddities and quirks aside, these organisations tend to operate in similar ways, their victims make the same blunders.

What possesses an intelligent person to join a cult? That's what I wanted to know. But no one in this group was giving me answers.

When the next volunteer took her turn, I didn't expect much. By this point, my attention was focused on the clock on the wall as I waited for it to reach eight, when I could politely leave and never return. The volunteer told us her name – Lucy – and that she was a nurse, emphasising the past tense *was* – she'd lost her job. A nurse, like Julie had been.

I looked at her: a young woman with light brown hair, in her mid-thirties at most, perched on the edge of her chair, leaning forward, as though any moment she might bolt. Unlike the others, she spoke eloquently, recalling her experiences vividly, and I was soon drawn into her story, despite her coughing fits that frequently interrupted her flow. What excited me most was her description of the Cumbria retreat where she'd spent over a year, and the man who ran the place.

A few weeks later, we met in a café in Preston. As we sat down with our drinks – a latte for me, a bottle of spring water for Lucy – I thanked her again for agreeing to see me.

When the group meeting had come to an end, while everyone was gathering their coats and bags, I'd approached Lucy and told her about Julie, explaining how she'd been to the same retreat years ago. I asked if we might stay in touch. We exchanged a few emails before arranging to meet.

In the café, I told her about the book I'd started writing: an exposé of the cult practices that have been going on at the Blundale retreat for at least twenty years. I asked Lucy if she'd be willing to contribute her account.

I assured her, somewhat awkwardly, that I'm happily married; I want nothing from her besides her story. By getting the truth out there, I said, we might encourage other survivors to come forward; eventually, this will gather the momentum needed for police to pursue an investigation. That's how other cults have been stopped before. I told her I already had a publisher (who, admittedly, are expecting a rather different book, but I see no reason why they should not be interested in this new project) and handed her printed copies of my published articles, to attest to my quality as a writer.

Whether my spiel was ultimately persuasive, or Lucy has reasons of her own, I'm not certain – but she agreed.

Over the course of two months, Lucy recounted her experiences to me across multiple interviews, from which I have reconstructed her story, divided into six parts. I have made certain stylistic adjustments in converting audio transcripts into literary narrative form, endeavouring to achieve fluid prose while retaining an authentic sense of Lucy's voice. Her account is interspersed with selected transcripts from our recorded interviews, as well as my own additional material and research, that provide further illumination upon our subject.

Those wishing to read Lucy's original account, straight from the source, as it were, may skip to the full transcripts from our interview recordings in the appendix.[1]

---

1. **Editor's note:** The aforementioned full transcripts are missing from the author's manuscript.

Transcript Excerpt #1

ME: It's recording.
LUCY: Should I start?
ME: Yes, if you could introduce yourself.
LUCY: Okay. My name's Lucy. I'm here to talk about what goes on at the Hart Wellness Centre. I –

> *[A knocking interrupts us: three hard raps.]*

LUCY: *[SIGHS]* Sorry, just a minute.

> *[Her chair creaks as she gets up; she opens her door a crack. A man stands behind it. His facial features bear some similarity to Lucy's, but he looks slightly older; his hair is the same shade of light brown, mottled with grey. For half a second, he stares directly into the camera and his eyes meet mine. He looks annoyed.]*

MAN: What you doing?

LUCY: I'm on Skype. What is it?

MAN: We're nipping out. Can you watch the girls?

LUCY: Not right now, I'm in a meeting.

MAN: *[snorts]* What sort of meeting?

LUCY: With someone from my support group.

MAN: *[stops smirking]* Oh, right. Can you do that another time?

LUCY: Can you just give me half an hour? It's important.

MAN: *[sighs]* Alright.

> *[Lucy shuts the door and returns to her chair, her head and shoulders in view once more. She has dark circles under her eyes. Behind her is her door and a whitewashed wall, upon which hangs a painting of a mountain.]*

LUCY: Sorry about that.

ME: Was that your brother?

LUCY: Yeah. He assumes I'm always available to babysit my nieces. *[She coughs.]* Sorry, one sec. *[She splutters, breaking into a coughing fit.]*

> *[Lucy mutes her microphone and silently coughs into her fist. She picks up a mug and sips from it, then unmutes her mic.]*

LUCY: Sorry about that. Where were we?

ME: How about starting with how you ended up there? Why join a cult?

Lucy

WE'RE ON THE MOUNTAIN summit, a circle of us in Lotus Pose. Sun beating down. Our hair whips our faces in the warm breeze, our bums and legs are sore from sitting on the rocks. We're supposed to close our eyes, press our palms on the ground. Focus. But my friend, Faith, sitting next to me, keeps lifting one hand to scratch a rash on her arm. I can hear her doing it.

A few of us have developed these rashes lately, or red, itchy eyes. Diarrhoea, vomiting. We're told the rashes are our toxic thoughts rising to the surface of our bodies, to be shed like snakeskin, or cried out, defecated, purged. We're told this is a natural, healthy process.

No one raises concerns about bathing in Murkwater down in the valley. Since the start of summer, the north basin of the lake, which is closest to the retreat, has turned bright green, as though someone spilled a vat of paint across its surface. Deep down in some inaccessible part of myself, I know this stuff is blue-green algae. When I was still a nurse, I'd treated a little boy who'd been admitted to hospital with severe gastroenteritis after swimming in a reservoir and swallowing the water.

But if this idea rises to the top of my cloudy consciousness for a second, I stamp it back down. That's toxic thinking. I worry the treacherous thought has written itself across my face, and someone in the group will open their eyes and see how corrupt I am. How unhealthy.

No one can be unhealthy here.

It's not possible when we're living in this sacred place, under the generous guidance of Charles, our Master Healer. His skin is clear and smooth, rash-free, golden-tanned instead of sunburned like the rest of us. He's sitting on my right, calling out for Michael to bless us, channelling the mountain's healing energy to everyone in the circle. I'm trying to concentrate on Charles saving us, but I'm distracted by the frantic rhythm of Faith's fingernails scraping back and forth across skin. I open my eyes a fraction and see her arm: its constellation of bumps and blisters, scratch marks, smears of blood.

I want her to stop before someone notices. Before anyone suspects the treatment's not working on her the way it should. The problem can't be the treatment. It must be her.

Even though she's supposed to be my friend, if she goes down, I'm not going down with her. I'm determined to stay at the retreat. I'm determined to heal.

It's all I care about anymore.

Since I got out, I've thought about that moment a lot. Asked myself how I ended up like that.

You think something like this could never happen to you, and that's exactly how they get to you.

When people find out I've been in a cult, something changes in their eyes. Suddenly, they're reassessing me, on the lookout for personality flaws, signs of whatever childhood trauma fucked me up. It's only through going to our support group that I've realised we're just ordinary people. Each of us has a different story.

I didn't come from a broken home. I was privileged. My therapist says there's a difference between parents attending to material needs and emotional needs, but I don't know. They had their hands full with my brother – Mark had problems at school, kept getting into trouble – plus they had stressful jobs, working long hours. I made sure I came home from school with glowing reports and gold stars. I kept out of their way. They'd say, 'At least we don't have to worry about you, Lucy.' As a kid, it was a huge compliment, being more mature than my older brother.

Faith and I latched onto one another in primary school. Each break time, we'd slink off together, just the two of us. I liked the warmth of her arm linked in mine, how she told everyone I was her best friend. I didn't mind her talking over me and bossing me around, deciding what games we played and which bands and TV shows were our favourites. Most of the time.

Whenever we fell out, I'd wander around the edge of the playground alone, while Faith strode up to some of the other girls and joined their skipping game or teamed up with the boys playing football. She didn't seem to need me at all. But I also knew that other kids laughed at her behind her back. At how she cried every morning after her mum dropped her off and disappeared through the school gates. At the ridiculous stories she made up about her dad when other kids asked where he was, why he didn't live with her – when she told everyone it was because he was a secret agent like James Bond, or the actual Phil Collins touring the world with Genesis. Sometimes kids remarked on how much I put up with being her friend, and I felt a twinge of victory. Awful, I know.

Back then, our fallouts didn't last long. By the time I'd worked up the courage to approach another kid on the playground and play with them instead, Faith would come looking for me. After we'd hugged and made up, she'd say she loved me, that I'd never let her down. I thought I never would.

During high school, we sat next to each other every lesson, went to each other's houses after school, every weekend. Whenever Faith came over, we stayed in my bedroom, playing *SimCity* on my computer, or play-acting as sister-duo witches, deep space explorers, demon-hunters. We'd only venture out for snacks from the kitchen. Once, Mark was there, sitting on the countertop, looming over us, refusing to move his legs blocking the cupboard where the crisps were. He smirked when we gave up trying to get them.

'Why are you two always together? Are you les-bians?'

He mimed being sick, then burst out laughing at his own joke, kicking the heels of his muddy trainers into the cupboard door Mum had just wiped clean.

Faith told him to fuck off, and we ran upstairs and barricaded my bedroom door before he could catch us. We both thought he was a dickhead.

Until then, I'd felt totally at ease cuddling Faith, holding hands. It was like stretching or breathing – I didn't think twice about it. Was it wrong for us to be this close? Nobody at school was gay – at least, no one admitted they were. I was the only girl in our year who hadn't had a boyfriend yet, who'd never even been kissed. I was too shy to ask anyone out, and if anyone tried to approach me, Faith gave them the brush-off. She'd had a few boyfriends, although they never last-ed long, didn't seem to mean that much to her. I'd invented a boyfriend or two to save face: someone I'd met on holiday, who didn't go to the same school. Kids canvassed other kids about their level of sexual experi-ence and ranked them. With boys, it only went in one direction: the more you had, the more respect you got. Girls had to be careful: too little meant you were frigid, too much made you a slut.

In Sixth Form, Faith and I weren't in the same class-es anymore. She did Drama, English, Music. I picked all the sciences because my parents said these were the safest options. Most of Sixth Form had stayed on from high school, but there were a couple of new kids. One of them was Nate, a tall, dark-haired boy with a tiny triangle of beard beneath his lower lip. He was in all my classes.

Biology was my favourite subject. I loved learning about nature and how my body worked. Nate and I got paired up for a project on culturing bacteria. He seemed nice and easy to talk to. He looked straight in my eyes when I spoke, as though he really cared about what I had to say. He was trying to decide between becoming an engineer, like his dad wanted, or a vet.

I wanted to be a nurse. A few months earlier, my dad had been hospitalised with pneumonia. Visiting him in hospital had been terrifying, seeing him hooked up to so many machines, a tube down his throat, his face ashen. But I liked the nurses. Their efficiency and verve as they flitted around the ward, stopping for a friendly word with each patient. How they relieved the pain in my dad's chest and made him laugh, even in that state. Their combination of skill and compassion was powerful. Focusing on them took my mind off how thin and weak my dad had become.

I was surprised when Nate asked me out. I'd thought his friendliness and ease meant that he couldn't possibly be interested in me, not like that. He was good-looking, intelligent, confident – he could have his pick of girl-friends – but he chose me. When I rushed to tell Faith, though, she looked disgusted.

'Why did you say yes? You barely know him.'

Her reaction was so cutting, I almost broke up with him in our next lesson. But it seemed like my only chance to have a boyfriend like everyone else.

As the weeks went by, she kept finding new reasons to hate him.

'Why does he grow that bum fluff on his chin? It looks like a Brazilian.'

She'd done this kind of thing before: mocked the things I liked and she didn't. She refused to hang out with him. 'I just can't. He's too boring.' She'd say it deliberately loud enough for him to hear. She wasn't impressed when I told her about our first kiss, or him saying he was in love with me.

'Oh, Luce. You're so gullible.'

I didn't want to argue with her, especially not when our time together was becoming more limited, with Nate asking to meet up after school and at the weekends – another reason Faith thought he was bad news.

'Surprise, surprise,' she said on the phone, after I'd told her I couldn't see her because I'd already made plans with Nate. 'With the boyfriend again.'

I hung up on her. I couldn't deal with the hostility in her voice, the effort to explain myself.

'She's a bitch,' said Nate. He'd called a few minutes later, while I was upset, and I ended up telling him what happened. 'She's toxic. Just tell her you don't want to be friends anymore.'

He sounded exasperated. He couldn't understand why I was her friend. On the few occasions I'd made plans with her instead of him, he'd sulked for hours.

Things were already bad enough for him, he'd said, with his control freak dad on his back, and on top of that, it was clear I didn't love him as much as he loved me.

At the time, this didn't seem manipulative. It seemed understandable he'd hate Faith after the way she'd treated him, and I felt horrible for making him feel worse.

If, on some level, I saw Faith had a point – that Nate was taking over my life – I didn't know what to do about it. It was the one thing in my life that was going well. Dad was still off work and didn't seem to be getting better, his horrible hacking cough reverberating through the house. Keeping up with my schoolwork was getting harder, and Mum worried about my suffering grades, about me ending up like Mark – no job, no prospects. I'd become detached from myself. Maybe it was the intense anxiety I'd been feeling since I'd started on the pill but was too embarrassed to talk about. Maybe teenagers just do stupid shit like this – and not just teenagers, I found out years later. I watched myself being buried under rubble, not knowing how to reach down and pull myself back out. There was only Nate surrounding me on all sides.

I was too much of a coward to confront Faith the way Nate wanted. What I did instead was worse. I acted like she didn't exist anymore: not calling her back, not speaking to her, avoiding eye contact with her at school. If I looked her way and she saw me, I turned away or pretended to look through her. Other girls rallied around her, giving me dirty looks across the canteen.

Nate told me to ignore them. 'We don't need anyone else.'

We were already planning our lives together after school: going to the same university in London – the university where his dad wanted him to study engineering, while I'd study nursing – and sharing a flat. Whether I really wanted any of this didn't seem to matter.

I don't know if I saw the signs then, or if I'm superimposing what I found out much later onto my memories: Faith getting thinner, paler. Dark circles under her eyes. A shadow on her neck. If I noticed anything, I told myself not to care. We were enemies.

Towards the end of our final year, Faith was absent from school, missing her A-Level exams. A rumour went round that she'd been in hospital, but I didn't ask anyone to confirm. I was too ashamed and nervous to get back in contact with her.

During the summer, while I was packing my stuff, getting ready to move out, I got an email from her.

I've been ill. I really need to talk to you. Can we meet up? Just the two of us.

Nate read the email over my shoulder, glaring at the computer monitor.

'She's lying. Guilt-tripping you,' he said. 'You know what she's like.'

He reminded me about all the packing that still needed doing, and I closed the email.

I never replied.

In the support group, we often talk about Hell. A guy who escaped a Christian fundamentalist sect told us he used to believe Hell was a literal place: fire, demons, pitchforks. A cesspit where the worst torture was reserved for traitors who'd left the church.

There's a different kind of hell. It's mundane, drab, indistinguishable from normal life. In 2011, the year before I went to the retreat, it was the tiny staff room in the hospital where, if I was lucky, I paused for breath during shifts, sipping scalding tea as fast as possible next to the sour-smelling fridge, before returning to chaos. It was the fluorescent strip lighting that glared over the corridors where, increasingly, patients were being left on trolleys for hours, wailing for help, soiling themselves. It was the visitors who shouted at my colleagues and me, spit flying from their mouths, demanding to know why their loved ones had been left in such a state. It was another sleepless night before a twelve-hour shift, the trudge from car park to hospital, back to the onslaught. One last glimpse of sky before heading inside.

Going home was even worse. I'd arrive late, hours after my shift was supposed to have ended. Nate would be sitting in stony silence on his PlayStation, or in bed already – he'd stopped bothering to wait up for me. He didn't want to hear my excuses anymore: how I couldn't have left work on time because there'd been an emergency with a patient, I'd had so much paperwork to do, I was covering for a colleague. He'd say, 'You care about your job more than me.' On the few days we had off work together, we'd tiptoe around one another, throwing out ideas for things we might do – we never made plans anymore – that neither of us could agree on, before ending up vegetating in front of the TV, wordlessly. Or we'd argue. Sometimes I think we argued just to fill the time.

Eventually, the pressure broke us.

Nate kept the flat in London, and I moved back North. My parents had both died a few years earlier. Dad got lung cancer, after years of chronic bronchitis. The day before Mum died, she'd gone to her GP, complaining of nausea and back pain, and was told it was just flu, to go home and put her feet up. The GP missed the signs of her heart attack. Mark lived close by, but we weren't in contact. He was angry at me for not visiting more often before our parents died, while he'd been their golden child, taking Dad to his hospital appointments, picking up his medication, helping Mum with shopping and housework. He'd conveniently forgotten the years of stress he'd put them through, before he turned his life around and started his own business.

I got a job in a hospice. I'd considered packing in nursing altogether, but I didn't know what else to do, and it felt easier to sidestep than retrain in something else. Dad had died in a hospice, and it seemed less chaotic than the hospital. It was, although it was draining in a different way. The lack of hope. The constant smell of death.

It was around then when the symptoms started. I'd be at work, speaking to a patient, checking their vitals – routine stuff – when my throat would suddenly tighten. An invisible hand clenching my windpipe. I'd start coughing, gasping for air.

It was alarming for the patients. Their family members would ask my colleagues, 'Should she be here? She could be infectious.'

I went to my GP to get it checked out. He found no sign of anything infectious. No sign of anything wrong at all. I told him it was affecting my work, that I couldn't even walk upstairs without setting it off. After every coughing fit, I felt exhausted. There had to be something wrong.

I spent hours in waiting rooms, months on waiting lists. I had a throat swab, a laryngoscopy, an X-ray, an MRI scan, and held on for the results: a telltale swelling, a tumour. The tests all came back clear. I spoke to ENT specialists, gastroenterologists, and oncologists – they didn't find anything. A simple acknowledgement that there was a problem from just one of them would have been nice.

Back in my GP's office, I asked what else he could do.

He pushed a leaflet about mental health services across his desk. 'Have you thought about counselling?'

I wanted to scream.

Instead, I said nothing, took the leaflet, and left, tossing it in the bin on my way out. When I got outside, I doubled over, coughing.

I went on sick leave, barely left my flat, barely slept. I googled my symptoms, scouring the internet for answers, obsessing over potential causes. Living near main roads. Eating junk food. Drinking. All those long, stressful shifts at the hospital. I'd brought it on myself, fucked everything up. Look how things ended with Nate. Look what I'd done to Faith.

Adverts for essential oils, supplements, and diets kept popping up on my screen. I'd always been sceptical of this stuff. I'd had patients who'd been rushed into hospital because their herbal remedies had interfered with their medications. Patients who were worried about vaccines yet had no problem taking supplements every day, even when they couldn't name a single ingredient in them. Anything like that used to make me roll my eyes and think: scam. It used to frustrate me, how people were so ready to distrust medicine but believe in miracles.

Then medicine let me down, and I ended up clicking on those adverts.

I tried juicing. Yoga. I bought a rose quartz pebble from a website that said it would mend broken hearts and promote healing. The smooth baby-pink crystal lived on my bedside table, and I'd gaze at it before drifting off to sleep. I wasn't convinced these things would actually work, but I didn't think they'd do any harm either. Before, all the juice gave me diarrhoea.

When I wasn't googling, I was scrolling through Facebook, where I had hundreds of 'friends'. No one I felt comfortable reaching out to for support.

Over the years, I'd occasionally typed Faith's name in the search bar. None of the profiles that came up looked like the girl I remembered. Even if I'd found her on there, I wasn't brave enough to send a friend request. What if she ignored it, or only accepted to send me abuse? Best case scenario, all was forgiven, but that didn't mean we'd be on the same wavelength anymore. Part of me was desperate to speak to her, be close to her again.

Another part was afraid of her.

One day, a new friend request popped up in my notifications. When I saw her name, my heart stopped. It triggered a coughing fit.

Sometimes it's hard to tell the difference between excitement and dread: both hit you with the same adrenaline rush.

There was no message with her request – no explanation why she wanted to reconnect with me. I couldn't ignore it. I had to know more. My hand trembled as I clicked to accept.

I expanded her profile picture. She had the same wide forehead and pointed chin, mole on her neck, green eyes with long, naturally curling eyelashes I used to secretly covet while I struggled with an eyelash curler. Those familiar features had been displaced onto a different woman. I drank in her clear, glowing skin, her huge smile with whitened teeth. The biggest change was her hair – sleek and brown, kissing her shoulders, nothing like the waist-length blonde mane she used to have.

I gathered, searching through her timeline, she ran an online business selling crystals. Along with posting photos of the crystals, she included descriptions of their healing properties, the energies they radiated. She was either a good salesperson or took her work seriously. I followed a link to her website, saw the listing for rose quartz. The same one I'd bought. When the crystal arrived in the post, my name and address had been handwritten on the parcel. I'd thought the handwriting seemed familiar. Had she recognised my name?

There was a photo of her in a restaurant with her arm around an older woman. Sandra, her mum, whose face had a lean, pinched look it never used to have. She was wearing a blue head scarf, so I guessed she'd lost her hair from cancer treatment. Faith had cleared her plate, but Sandra had barely touched her pasta. The date on the photo was from eighteen months earlier. I couldn't find any more recent photos of them together.

Faith didn't post anything for while. Then, six months later, she shared a photo of her reflection in a mirror. She wore gym leggings and a sports bra, revealing her flat stomach. She was holding up her phone to take the photo while holding the tree pose, the sole of her right foot resting on her left inner thigh, perfectly balanced. There was a caption with the photo.

Healthier than ever after an amazing stay at Hart Wellness Centre!

She posted photos of fells and lakes in Cumbria, although none of the retreat itself. A photo of a book with a red cover.

This book is INCREDIBLE. Reading Toxic People *changed my life!*

People had commented on how good she looked. I wasn't sure whether it was appropriate to 'like' any of her photos or add a comment. Still, she was the one who'd added me, who'd offered an olive branch.

I took the plunge and commented on her profile photo: *Wow, Faith, you look great! Hope all is well with you.* I debated for a good ten minutes whether to add a kiss on the end.

Shortly after, she messaged me directly.

We met at a coffee shop.

I spotted her through the window, queuing up. She didn't see me at first. Her fingers hovered over the packets of crisps. She picked up a pre-packaged sandwich from the fridge section, then tossed it back as though it had burned her. In the end, she only grabbed a bottle of water.

My heart was racing as I tapped her on the shoulder. When she turned to face me, the tense expression on her face vanished almost immediately, replaced with a beaming smile.

She threw her arms around me, and I felt how slight she was. She smelled like fresh herbs – lavender and chamomile.

'It's so good to see you.'

Her tone sounded genuine. I swallowed hard, trying not to cry, but when she pulled away, her eyes were brimming with tears. We burst out laughing.

While waiting for my coffee, we raised our voices above the hiss of the espresso machine, the blare of other people's chatter and the radio.

'I still can't get over me buying one of your crystals without realising,' I said. I'd already mentioned this when we'd been messaging each other. 'Did you know it was me?'

'I recognised your name, obviously. I wasn't certain it was you.'

I wanted to ask if that's what prompted her to find me on Facebook, but she changed the subject, asking how my job was going.

We found a table and sat down. She reminded me how I used to put E45 on her back when her eczema was bad. The time she fell over skateboarding and I dabbed her bruises with witch hazel.

'The nursing thing makes sense. You always had paracetamol in your bag in case someone had a headache.'

I'd forgotten about that. My 'stash'.

She asked if I remembered us wearing matching outfits on non-uniform day.

'Oh, god,' I said, 'why would you remind me about that?'

We'd gone through a phase of wearing the same clothes. My parents thought it was weird, but Sandra said it was sweet. When she bought a new top for Faith, she bought an extra one for me.

I asked Faith how Sandra was doing, and the smile slid off her face. She said her mum had Stage 3 endometrial cancer and was about to start her second round of chemotherapy. She paused, and I waited for her to carry on when she was ready. At the hospice, I'd learned to resist jumping in with words like hope and bravery when talking about cancer.

'It's been awful,' she said. 'Watching her suffer. And it's brought it all back to me, what I went through. Chemo at eighteen. Not fun.'

My stomach dropped. I tried not to show it as I put the pieces together in my mind. Her absence from school. The hospitalisation rumours. Her email.

I've been ill. I really need to talk to you.

I hadn't known, not properly, but I'd had my suspicions. Rather than seeking confirmation, I'd shut myself off, preferring ignorance to truth.

Our eyes met over the table, and I couldn't quite read the look she gave me.

She dropped her gaze and went on talking as though I hadn't ghosted her, as though there'd never been an email – even though I knew it, she knew it. Was she trying to make things easier for me or protecting herself?

It's easier to pretend people you love aren't capable of doing horrible things to you.

It had started with a lump in her neck. Waking up at night in a pool of her own sweat and being so exhausted the next day she couldn't get out of bed to go to school. Her doctor confirmed it was Hodgkin Lymphoma and told her she'd need chemotherapy, then radiotherapy.

'No one discussed other options,' she said, her voice quivering. 'No one gave me a choice.'

I wanted to ask: what other choice was there?

I kept my mouth shut.

'I had no idea what I was getting myself in for. I mean, I knew it'd make me throw up and my hair would fall out, but knowing something and it actually happening to you isn't the same thing.'

After treatment, she learned about the long-term effects of chemotherapy and radiotherapy on the body.

'I already knew chemo might make me infertile because they froze my eggs. But there were other things no one warned me about.'

She listed them: nerve damage, a tingling in her hands that never went away. Fatigue. Brain fog. Increased risk of secondary cancers.

'I was like, what, this so-called therapy might give me more cancer? Wonderful. Perfect. I've tried to counteract it with clean eating, yoga, crystals and stuff. But the worry never goes away. Every time I feel pain anywhere, I think the cancer's back.'

She let out a shaky sigh and tipped her bottle to her mouth too forcefully, spilling water on her lap. I passed her my napkin, and she carried on talking as she blotted herself dry.

'While Mum was having her first round of chemo, I found a lump. Same place as last time.'

My eyes went straight to her neck, which appeared smooth, normal. She laughed.

'Don't worry, I'm fine now. But they said it was cancer. Just my luck.'

The words tumbled out of my mouth before I could stop them. 'But you look so healthy!'

She smiled, folding the wet napkin into a neat square.

'Thank you. I feel healthy. Finally.'

'How long was the treatment?'

'Oh, I didn't have their *treatment*. I said, "There's no way I'm going through chemo again." They thought I was insane. They didn't understand I'd spent ten years trying to rebuild my life, my identity.' She ran her fingers through her hair, so much finer and darker than it used to be. 'I learned to love my new hair, after it grew back different. I'm not losing it again.'

I tried to absorb what she was telling me. 'I don't understand. How did you get rid of the cancer?'

She leaned forward in her seat. Her face lit up.

'There's this health retreat in the Lake District. Luce, it's incredible. It cured me.'

'Oh, really?' I fought to hide my kneejerk scepticism.

'They use all-natural healing methods. I've got this book that explains the process. I'll lend it to you.'

All-natural healing methods? I wasn't sure I wanted to know what that meant. I sipped my coffee and took a bite of my pastry. Was her cancer really in remission? Or was it still lurking under her skin, unchecked?

'I'm trying to get Mum to go.' Her voice broke, her smooth features suddenly distorted with frustration. 'Apparently, she feels safer pumping her body full of toxic chemicals. Completely brainwashed.'

Again, I didn't know what to say.

Faith sighed and changed the subject, asking after my own parents.

I told her they'd both died. She said how sorry she was, how it must have been devastating.

'And Nate leaving you on top of all that.'

That made me flinch – her presumption that our separation hadn't been my decision.

I swallowed my pride, let her statement go uncorrected. Okay, she'd been tactless, but she was trying to be sympathetic. Wasn't she? Maybe it was my imagination, but she'd sounded a little smug. Across her lips was the faintest flicker of 'told you so'.

A burn at the back of my throat. At first it felt like acid reflux, until I couldn't breathe. I looked down at my half-eaten pastry, thinking I must have taken a bite without realising and now it was lodged in my windpipe.

I knocked over my coffee cup as I jumped to my feet, my hands fluttering at my throat. Everyone stared. This is it, I thought. I'm going to die. Faith was at my side, slapping me hard on the back to help me spit out whatever I was choking on.

Except I wasn't choking on anything. Once again, my body had gone haywire.

It passed as quickly as it came. Within a few seconds, I was breathing normally again, although the inside of my throat still felt raw. I kept coughing. Faith helped me back into my chair and got me a water. While she mopped up spilled coffee, I sipped my water, spluttering, trying to ignore the people looking at me.

Faith leaned over. 'You okay?'

'Fine. Just embarrassed.'

'You don't look fine.'

In truth, I felt awful. Like iron weights had been strapped across my body. My skin was covered in a film of cold sweat. I was shivering.

She wrapped her jacket around my shoulders and asked what had happened. I filled her in on the months of inconclusive GP visits and hospital appointments, how it wasn't contagious. Most people kept their distance, just in case. Faith was different. She pulled her chair up close to mine. While I spoke, she nodded and listened attentively, full of sympathy and concern. I was touched by that, but also on my guard for her smugness to creep back – she was the picture of health.

Instead, her expression grew excited. She put her hand on mine.

'You know that retreat I mentioned earlier? I'm going back soon. Come with me!'

'I'll think about it,' I said, wary of committing myself to anything.

'You should have seen me before I went, Luce. I was a mess. Then I read *Toxic People*, and it completely changed my outlook on what illness is. I'll lend it you. Anyway, the guy who wrote it runs this retreat, and I thought, what have I got to lose? Might as well give it a try. Now I just wish I'd known about it when I was eighteen.'

I promised her I'd look into it. The retreat sounded too good to be true, although, admittedly, I was intrigued. Still, I wasn't sure how I'd manage with my cough away from home when getting coffee was challenging enough. I also wasn't sure how I felt about going with Faith. Something felt off.

Even when we'd been best friends, she'd never been this nice to me.

When I got home, she texted me.

Hope you're feeling better. Let me know if you're up for the retreat!

I looked it up online. Tried, anyway. There were no Google reviews, no TripAdvisor or Facebook pages. As though it didn't exist. For a moment, I wondered if Faith had made it up – a cruel practical joke to get my hopes up and lead me astray. Revenge for abandoning her all those years ago. But this didn't tally with her texting every day over the following weeks to ask how I was, if I needed anything, offering to bring homemade soup. Whenever I checked my phone, there'd be at least one text from her, sometimes a missed call. It started getting on my nerves, but I knew I ought to be grateful. It had been a long time since anyone had shown me this much care and attention.

'They don't really *do* reviews,' she said. I'd called her back and asked why there was hardly any information about the retreat online. 'You couldn't really put a star rating on what they do. You have to experience it for yourself.'

I found that odd. How did they promote themselves as a business?

Then I came across the celebrity endorsements on Goop. A TV star said the retreat helped him overcome drug addiction. A supermodel-turned-wellness entrepreneur claimed it cured her breast cancer. Neither explained how. Both said Charles Hartman was the smartest man they'd ever met, Blundale the most beautiful place on earth. The article called the retreat: *the Lake District's best kept secret*.

The retreat had a website – mostly photos of its impressive location beneath a mountain, a manor house, with a grand entrance hall. There was a list of package rates, a booking form, and a page to order Charles's book, but little information otherwise.

The retreat's proximity to outstanding natural beauty will leverage your cells' regenerative properties, while expert healers will unlock your body's inherent propensity to self-heal.

There was something evasive about those vague, appealing words; something that escaped scrutiny. Then again, maybe I was being overly dismissive. My nurse's instincts kicking in, priming me to roll my eyes at the idea of natural healing, though I hadn't given it a chance.

I invited Faith over for a film night – the first time I'd had a friend over at my new flat. It was nice to do something fun and normal, to pretend I wasn't avoiding going out in case I had another public coughing fit. Faith was my friend again, and it felt like slipping into an old jumper I hadn't worn in years, although it wasn't as cosy as I remembered. When I opened the door and she squealed and kissed me on the cheek, I couldn't shake this feeling that she was faking it.

Why did she want to be friends again? After what I'd done to her.

She handed me a flowery Get Well Soon gift bag, a copy of *Toxic People* inside. She clapped excitedly as I glanced over the blurb and the black-and-white author photo: a long-haired, bearded man, pale eyes framed by a pair of 70s aviator glasses.

She didn't touch the popcorn I'd made. She kept talking over the film about her favourite parts of *Toxic People*, or her upcoming trip to the retreat.

'Have you decided if you're coming yet?' A nervous edge to her voice, a pleading look in her eyes.

'I'd love to,' I lied, 'but it's too expensive.' My eyes had watered when I saw the prices on their website.

'I'm such an idiot. I should've said. I can get you a discount. Recommend a friend scheme. You'll get, like, fifty percent off.'

'That would be amazing.'

'It really is worth every penny, Luce.' She must have heard my lingering hesitation. 'If it doesn't work, it doesn't work. At least you'll get away for a week. It's absolutely stunning there.'

A holiday was tempting. It had been years since I'd gone away – I was always either too busy working or off sick. Nate got so tired of it, he'd started doing solo trips.

'But what if it did work,' she said. 'Imagine getting your life back without that cough. Isn't it worth a shot?'

Her words struck a chord. I didn't want to stay like this: too sick to work, practically housebound. Constantly feeling pathetic. Broken.

'You're right,' I said. 'What have I got to lose?'

Faith sorted the booking and transport, despite me offering to drive us.

'Cars aren't allowed onsite,' she said, 'not even taxis. You have to get the train and then they pick you up in the minivan. Minimises pollution,' she added, seeing the questioning look on my face.

Faith booked the minivan to pick us up in Penrith, and we agreed to meet at Manchester Piccadilly. When I arrived, I spotted her beneath the Departures board, carrying only a small handbag, while I'd broken a sweat heaving my holdall from the taxi. She didn't see me at first – she kept looking in the wrong direction. She looked anxious.

When she saw me, she jogged over.

'What took you so long?'

'Stuck in traffic,' I said, taken aback by how annoyed she sounded.

'Sorry. I thought you'd stood me up.'

Her laughter sounded forced.

'Which platform are we on?' I wanted to slip past the awkwardness, my sudden flood of guilt. Her fear of being stood up probably stemmed from how I'd treated her in the past.

'Come on, it's leaving in a minute.' She marched off ahead, and I struggled to keep up. She kept looking over her shoulder and mouthing, 'Hurry!'

She only relaxed when we were on the train. After lifting my holdall onto the luggage rack, out of breath from running, my throat and chest were on fire. I started coughing. She gave me her water, which I sipped as the train sped away from the city.

I thought she'd be buzzing. The previous night, she'd texted to say she couldn't wait for our trip. Now we were on our way, she was quiet. She slumped back in her seat, staring out the window. I asked if everything was okay. She didn't hear me at first, zoned out.

'I started reading *Toxic People* last night,' I said, thinking it might reanimate her.

'Oh, yeah?'

She sounded bored, even slightly hostile, as though she'd wanted to be left alone with her thoughts. Her phone vibrated on the table, and I spotted the caller's name as the screen lit up: *Mum*. She snatched up her phone and stuffed it in her bag.

'It's really interesting,' I said. In truth, I'd skimmed a few paragraphs of the introduction and given up. Vague, empty phrases, like the retreat's website.

Faith didn't hear me. That anxious expression I'd caught earlier was back on her face.

'Everything okay?'

'Fine.'

She wouldn't meet my eyes.

I tried another tack and asked how her crystal business was going, but she just shrugged. Maybe it wasn't going that well at all, so I dropped the subject.

The noise blaring all around – humming engine, automated voice announcing the next stop – amplified the silence between us. I racked my brain for something else to talk about and found myself wondering what we had in common.

I was relieved to get off the train at Penrith a couple of hours later. Tourists armed with rucksacks and picnic bags swarmed out of the station. We stood at the taxi rank without speaking, looking across the road at the ruins of a castle.

A white minivan pulled up, and a burly man with a ginger beard got out. His grey linen pyjamas reminded me of a Buddhist monk, incongruous with his sunglasses. He whistled and spun the car key around his index finger as he swaggered towards us.

'Back again,' he said, smirking at Faith. 'Your pledge?'

He nodded in my direction. I didn't know what he was talking about, so I looked at Faith, expecting her to laugh at some in-joke, but she didn't even smile. She turned bright red.

I pretended not to notice and introduced myself. The driver shook my hand and told me his name was Noah.

'I'm sure Faith's told you all about our little family.'

'I haven't told her anything,' she said, glaring at him. He chuckled to himself and turned towards another person stood nearby, a black woman in her late forties or early fifties. She leaned on a walking stick made of glittery pink plastic. Her glasses and nail polish were the same Barbie pink.

'Esther, is it?' he asked her. 'Another newcomer.'

He opened the sliding door and helped Esther climb inside. I sat next to her, and Faith followed and sat on my other side. Noah whistled again as he got back in the driver's seat and fired up the engine.

Esther asked us where we'd travelled from. I was surprised she'd come all the way from Bristol.

Noah piped up from the front: 'We get people from all over the world.'

His accent sounded local. I asked if he came from Cumbria.

'Barrow, originally. But Blundale's my home. I've been at the retreat for thirty years.'

I guessed he must be at least fifty if he'd started working there in the eighties, but he looked around forty at most.

Esther glanced over at Noah before leaning towards me and Faith, lowering her voice as she asked what we knew about the retreat. 'I've got arthritis. I've heard this place performs miracles.' She raised one eyebrow, as though she'd have to see it to believe it. Then she shrugged. 'I'll try anything at this point.'

I glanced at Faith, expecting her to repeat what she'd told me about the retreat curing her cancer. She wasn't paying attention to us, tapping away on her phone instead. I didn't think it was my place to share her story, so I told Esther about my chronic cough, how my doctor thought it was all in my head. She nodded sympathetically, saying it had taken her two years to get a diagnosis. 'My doctor didn't take me seriously for a long time. Didn't believe how much pain I was in. Might not have needed this, had I been diagnosed sooner.' She held up her walking stick.

Soon the fells rose above us on either side of the road, their rugged peaks and deep troughs stretching out into the distance. It was a relief to escape the city, where ugly buildings clogged up the skyline. Pockets of civilisation popped up here and there – sheep grazing on farmland, villages and hamlets crawling up the hills like ants.

We turned off the main road onto a narrow country lane. Noah didn't slow down, turning sharply at bends, plummeting down sudden drops like a rollercoaster. My stomach began to roil.

There were no vehicles on the road besides the minivan. No streetlamps or road signs, except for PRIVATE LAND, NO TRESPASSING signs. Trees crowded on either side. I grew dizzy with nausea, relieved when the minivan came to a stop outside a fenced off area with a padlocked gate.

Noah killed the engine. 'Won't be a minute.'

He got out and slammed the door behind him. The locks clicked.

Esther and I exchanged a look. Him locking up was an absent-minded, habitual thing, surely. Still, I didn't like it.

We watched him stroll towards the gate and pull a set of keys out of his pocket. He turned one of them inside the padlock.

Something had rolled out from under my seat when Noah hit the brake. I bent forward to get a closer look. A piece of rope, frayed at the edges.

A screech made me look up. Noah was pushing the gate open, the hinges seriously rusty. He got back in and steered us through the entrance, before locking up behind him. A CCTV camera stood on a pole beside the gate.

He got back in the driver's seat, flashing us a grin in the rear-view mirror.

'Almost there, ladies.'

My travel sickness began to wane as we went slowly uphill through dense woodland. I kept nudging the piece of rope with my shoe, until the view through the windscreen distracted me. A gap in the trees ahead, a brilliant white light bursting over the road.

'Wait till you see Lyfell Pike,' he said.

The trees fell away, and we broke into the light. All around was sunshine, blue sky, rolling hills, a yellow sea of daffodils.

'Feel that?'

I didn't know what he was talking about, until I clapped eyes on the mountain.

A tingle in the pit of my stomach, like a kid's excitement on Christmas Eve. A delicious shudder spreading through my legs and arms, up my spine. Somewhere inside me, a switch flicking.

Feeling more alive than I'd been in a long time.

I turned to Faith to see if she'd felt it, too. But she wasn't looking at the mountain – she had turned in her seat to stare at the trees, back the way we came.

The Magic Mountain

Originally published on 15 August 2006 on my now-defunct blog, Those Who Trespass.

Alas, we reach the last leg in our tour of my top five Lake District peaks. In case you missed it, read last week's post about my second favourite, Great Gable, <u>here</u>.

This post pays tribute to one of Cumbria's most underrated beauty spots: Lyfell Pike and the surrounding valley of Blundale. This area often gets overlooked by tourists, nestled as it is between some of the area's more popular landmarks – Helvellyn to the south, Ullswater to the east, Keswick to the west. All the better for those of us who crave a little solitude.

There is disagreement as to how Blundale got its name. Some place its etymology after the Norman conquest, comparing it to the Old French word 'blund', or fair-haired: in early spring, daffodils turn the valley golden-yellow. Others say Blundale was named by the Vikings invaders of Northumbria. In Old Norse, 'blunda' means to shut one's eyes or doze – according to legend, the secluded valley induces sleep, dreams, delusions.

Vikings have also been credited with naming Lyfell Pike, as derived from the Old Norse 'lyf', meaning life or medicine. People have long believed the mountain can heal the sick. Bede writes of a monastery at Blundale in 731 AD, where pestilence struck in the latter half of the 7th century. Not one of the monks succumbed to the disease that had decimated whole fiefdoms. Bede attributes this miracle to the holiness of Saint Michael, who climbed to the top of the mountain and fasted for forty days and forty nights, praying that his brethren might be spared. When Michael passed away at a ripe old age, he was first interred beneath the monastery until the monks decided to move him, fearing Viking raids. The monks carried his remains up the mountain, intending to build a shrine on the summit. They were never seen again. Historians have speculated the men perished on Knife Edge, a notoriously steep ridge, or possibly of hypothermia, although local legend has it that the monks wander still, their great brother having risen in his shroud.

Four centuries later, a local abbot wrote of Blundale Hall, a manor house built on the site of the ruined monastery, and the sickly, reclusive lord who occupied it. After one month in his new home, the lord of the manor grew hale and hearty. Gregarious in his newfound vitality, he held huge banquets, entertaining powerful men from across the country. Blundale Hall was rebuilt in 1677 and refurbished several times over the course of three centuries. It still stands today.

My revisit to Lyfell Pike is long overdue. Driving north along the A591 is, for me, a journey through time. Everywhere about me, I encounter echoes of the very first trip I made to the Lake District thirty-five years ago when I was seventeen, accompanied by three lads from school. There is Grasmere village in all its picture-postcard prettiness, cheerfully defying the turn of the twentieth century. On to Wythburn Church, where my friends and I once sought shelter from a downpour and tried to read the inscriptions on the lichen-greened gravestones. To my left, through trees, I glimpse the rippling waters of Thirlmere, into which decades of my life have dissolved. On, then, to Blundale, and the halcyon days of my youth.

Blundale's old pub, The Elixir, is where I tasted my first pint of real ale. Blundale Hall, a youth hostel at that time, is where I slept off my first hangover. At the edge of Murkwater, we sat and smoked, bathed our blistered feet, and watched trout meander below.

All of this was well and good, making memories to last a lifetime. Happy, irreverent moments to smile about years later and think, 'Yes, I have lived.' Then there are the sublime moments that change you, transform your perspective, alter the very fabric of your being. This, for me, was climbing Lyfell Pike.

Why has it taken me so many years to return to Lyfell Pike? I think it is because of fear. Fear that it's surely impossible to surpass or even come close to the feeling it once gave me. Fear that repetition would tarnish its magic and beauty and vividness in my memory.

At seventeen, I no longer believed in God. I sat through church only to make my mother happy, but found the teachings meaningless and, at worst, distasteful. I shudder to remember reciting catechism.

But when we reached the mountain's zenith, I found God – as good as, anyway, the nearest possible thing. I saw God with my own eyes, stretching out for miles and miles before me, in every recess and swell of land, in the lake mirroring the sky, in forests and fish and birds that thrived in all this harmonious balance, this celestial equilibrium.

God was never a silly story from an old book, a spectre invented by cynical minds to suppress and subdue. God was here all along: a place and a feeling, very much alive.

Now he returns: no longer a fresh-faced youth, this middle-aged academic, husband and father clocking on for fifty-two.

He is seeking something. Is it rejuvenation? Longevity? A miracle cure for the creeping onset of old age? Or something more essential: some inkling into the mystery that is life and his place in this world – which, as a man of science, he knows he may never grasp, or that there may be no answer to the mystery after all, and yet some ancestral, pre-Enlightenment residue in his DNA leads him to that mountain, searching.

He parks up and puts on his walking boots, then sets off on the footpath towards Little Heaven Gate, the scree slope where he will ascend the western side of Lyfell Pike. He feels trepidation. Wouldn't you, knowing you were about to face God? Worse still – what if he no longer finds God up there? He was only seventeen the first time, young and foolish. He only has his memories to trust, but now he knows memory is fickle and cannot be trusted.

But what's this? A high fence erected through the woods, a locked gate blocking the footpath he has diligently followed for two miles from Dowth Farm. There is no such obstruction indicated along the dotted line on his Ordnance Survey map – which, admittedly, is twenty years old (he makes a mental note to purchase the updated version). He spies a sign on a tree.

PRIVATE LAND

NO PUBLIC RIGHT OF WAY

He looks for another way in, but the fence stretches through the woods as far as he can see.

He decides to ignore the sign and climb over the gate. Within a few hundred yards, he is met with another notice more insistent than the first.

NO TRESPASSING

PRIVATE PREMISES

CCTV 24 HOURS

TRESPASSERS WILL BE PROSECUTED

Sure enough, at the top of a metal pole he finds a CCTV camera angling down at him. He stares back into its glass eye. He doesn't care who sees. He has a right to be here. This is the same route he took with his friends thirty-five years ago.

He walks on awhile through the woods, trying not to let the threat of prosecution distract him from his pilgrimage. He listens to the steady crunch of his boots on the gravel path, a sudden sound of beating wings as a bird launches off a branch overhead. A red squirrel scurries up a tree. He begins to feel strange, dizzy, and pauses to reach into his rucksack for a bottle of water.

Something moves between the trees – a glimpse of grey. A twig snaps. Footsteps approach, hastening. He stops and blinks a few times, for what he sees surely can't be real: two men in matching grey uniforms, running towards him, one brandishing a scythe.

Before he registers what is happening, he is running back in the direction he came.

He jumps over the gate with a litheness bestowed by adrenaline and sheer luck. He keeps on running, just once casting his eye over his shoulder to check the progress of his pursuers, who come no further than the gate and stand behind it, watching.

The scythe blade catches the sunlight and glints.

Later, while sipping a pint of dark mild in The Elixir, I debate whether or not to report my would-be attackers to the police. Ultimately, I decide against it. Technically, yes, I was trespassing, but that's not what concerns me. I'm not sure I'd be believed.

Their matching clothes intrigue me. Are they escapees from some sort of institution?

Not exactly: this is the uniform worn by staff of the Hart Health and Wellness Centre, the wizened proprietor of The Elixir tells me. Blundale Hall changed hands back in the late seventies when Charles Hartman, a bestselling author, bought the property and, subsequently, the surrounding land.

'Funny you should mention escapees,' the pub landlord says, wryly, as he pulls another pint. He hands me the drink and tells me several people have wound up here, over the years, dressed in the same grey uniform.

'They always look shaken up. Like they haven't eaten or slept in weeks. A young lady came here once, about thirteen years ago, begging to use the telephone. The only thing she had with her was a fountain pen. She left it behind when her taxi came. The pen didn't even work, the ink had dried up. But there was stuff on the nib. Looked like dried blood.'

'What happened to her?' I ask, mildly curious.

He shrugs. 'Didn't ask. I keep myself to myself. I'm just trying to keep this place going, you know. It's changed a lot round here – local businesses shutting down, people moving away. All because of him. Hartman.'

I conclude this love letter to Lyfell Pike on a bittersweet note: I waited years to revisit the magic mountain, only to be turned away, all because one rich, selfish man has created an access island guarded with monsters.

Now, only this wealthy landowner and patrons of his so-called 'wellness centre' are able to freely enjoy Lyfell Pike, when its beauty and benefits should be accessible to all.

It is shameful. It is sacrilege.

Transcript Excerpt #2

ME: So, the beauty of the place drew you in. I can understand that. Lyfell Pike's my favourite peak in the Lakes. I wrote about it on my blog.

LUCY: Did you feel it? When you went?

ME: Feel what?

LUCY: That burst of energy.

ME: *[PAUSE]* Might that have been the excitement of the holiday? You said yourself, it was long overdue.

LUCY: No, it was too intense for that. The euphoria.

ME: Mmm. *[PAUSE]* Anyway, you arrive at the retreat. Did you notice anything strange? It's just it seems obvious to me, from Julie's letters, even the first, something's not right.

LUCY: I've talked about this in support group. Missing

the red flags. *[PAUSE]* Weird stuff happened, but I looked the other way. I chose not to see.

Lucy

AT RECEPTION, WE WERE told to hand over all our belongings.

I didn't hear that at first. I was too busy looking around the entrance hall, taking it all in. The wooden beams arching across the ceiling like a giant ribcage. Paintings hung all over the oak-panelled walls, dozens of Lyfell Pikes. Some had a gold-tinted sky around the mountain, a halo. Or a glowing figure standing on the summit. More than anything else, my eyes were drawn to the eight-foot-tall batik tacked above the fireplace, its fabric dyed with psychedelic oranges and purples, so out-of-place; a portrait of a long-haired, bearded man with aviator glasses, just like the author photo on the back of *Toxic People*.

Charles Hartman, watching over us.

Faith nudged me. She was already lifting her stuff onto the reception desk. I'd meant to ask how she'd packed a week's worth of clothes in one small handbag, while my holdall was cutting off the circulation to my fingers. She switched off her phone and put it next to the bag. I'd watched her use her phone plenty of times, and I could've sworn it had a small crack at the bottom, but I must have been wrong because the screen was smooth, flawless.

I turned to the woman behind the desk. 'Sorry, we can't keep our phones?'

'Yes, angel, that's right. Guests enjoy the experience far more without all that distraction.'

Her voice had a firm edge that brook no argument, even though she smiled in an indulgent, motherly way. I couldn't tell whether her pixie cut was naturally white or dyed, if her wrinkles had been botoxed out or she had smooth, young skin. I read her name on the badge pinned to her grey top: Karma.

I looked at Faith for confirmation, but she was heading over to a group of people waving at her from velvet armchairs by the fireplace. All wore grey uniforms.

'What about my clothes?' I asked, as Karma beckoned for me to hand over my holdall. I gave it to her without thinking.

She placed a neatly folded pile of grey linen and a drawstring bag on the desk.

'Once you've settled in, please change into the vestments and pop your own clothes in the bag, then give that to us for safe keeping. We'll provide fresh vestments every day.'

I was about to ask about underwear, before I found a tank top and knickers stashed among the linen.

I didn't want to seem like a diva, so I gave my phone to Karma and took the vestments, then moved out of the way so Esther could move up in the queue. I stood off to one side, waiting for Faith. She was in a much better mood now she was here with the other guests, chirping hellos, giving hugs. I guessed she met them on her previous stay because she didn't introduce us. It reminded me of our fallouts back at school – the casual way she was ingratiating herself with another group, freezing me out.

I didn't get it. Things had been going well between us, on the whole, and she'd made a huge deal about doing this trip together. Since getting on the train, though, she'd been preoccupied. Done with me. I was baggage she'd left at reception and forgotten about.

A breeze blew through the open door, hitting me with a waft of spring blossom and fresh countryside air, mingled with something else. Something earthy and foul.

Esther's voice boomed over the group's chatter, the tinkle of wind chimes.

'Hand over my clothes? Are you having a laugh?'

I didn't catch Karma's response because I was suddenly lightheaded, shivery. Low blood sugar, maybe – I hadn't eaten anything for hours – or travel sickness creeping back. Or another flare-up. I braced myself for my chest to compress and throat to tighten, my deep, bone-rattling cough. People's looks of annoyance and revulsion.

A hand gently touched my arm, sending a shockwave through my body.

I wheeled around and came face-to-face with a man who'd stepped straight out of the batik portrait hanging behind him. Only, he'd scooped up his hair into a hipster bun, trimmed and oiled his beard. Swapped the giant 70s specs for some stylish horn-rimmed frames. He had the same barely-there smile, the same intense, pale blue eyes.

His eyes draw you in.

'It's wonderful to have you with us, Lucy. I'm Charles.'

His softly-spoken, measured tone made me want to listen carefully, but he also asked a lot of questions: how I was doing today, how my journey had been. He didn't give me chance to ask how he knew my name. While I answered, he nodded as if nothing interested him more than what I had to say. His hand was still on my arm, my skin tingling beneath. I didn't feel unwell anymore.

'Your first time at the retreat is very special,' he said. 'A lot of guests come back. Some never want to go home!'

He laughed, flashing a full set of strong teeth, bright white like his clothes.

If I hadn't known he founded the retreat in the late 70s, I'd have guessed he was in his thirties. Everything about him indicated a man in his prime. His dark hair, his lean, sinewy physique. His only blemish was a small scar on his mouth that made his top lip curl up when he spoke – a slight snarl.

He told me how he loved welcoming new guests, how much I'd benefit from the experience, how he couldn't wait to guide me through the process. Like an afterthought, he handed me an official-looking document and a pen, and said, 'Just sign along the dotted line.'

He kept on talking about the retreat, and I didn't want to seem rude by breaking eye contact, but I knew I shouldn't sign something without reading it first. The document was several pages long. I flicked through it while he spoke, stealing a glance at each page. One line said: *I agree not to discuss any therapies or treatments offered at the retreat with anyone outside it.*

He must have noticed my attention linger on that point, because he chuckled. 'I know it might seem a little strange, but the agreement's just a formality. We like guests to come without prior expectations. Guarantees the effectiveness of the treatment.'

Granted, I'd never been to a wellness retreat before, but I didn't think signing an NDA was standard practice. these documents in relation to dodgy legal settlements, harassment cases. Why hadn't Faith forewarned me?

What else had she not told me about this place?

She'd returned to my side and was looking at the document in my hands. 'Oh, yeah, all newcomers sign that.' She waved her hand dismissively, like it was nothing, then gave my shoulder a gentle squeeze. 'It's fine, Luce.'

Her smile diverted to Charles, who she gazed at beatifically, cheeks flushed. She wasn't the only one – the other guests who'd been sat by the fire were now hovering around us, swept up in Charles's gravitational pull.

Everyone stood watching, waiting for me to sign the document.

If I was bolder I might have refused to sign it, but I wasn't bold. I withered under scrutiny. I couldn't face the humiliation of backing out now, in front of everyone. If I let Faith down again, I risked losing her friendship for good. Plus, the trip was all paid for, non-refundable. And what if the treatment worked? I had to give it a chance.

I scribbled my name on the dotted line.

Our room had a lake view. I sat at the bay window as soon as we got in.

'Stunning,' I said, watching Murkwater sparkle under the sun.

'Isn't it,' said Faith. 'I love this room.' She'd already claimed the bed nearest the window and was laying out her vestments on the covers.

It took a moment for my eyes to adjust after gazing at the sunny view. I'd expected the room to be grand and richly furnished, like the entrance hall. But aside from the bay window and fancy ceiling cornices, it was drab, institutional – threadbare carpets, thin curtains. The cast iron bed frames made me think of hospitals from Victorian times, the kind used to prevent bed bugs. I walked over to the other bed and peeled apart the sheets. They had dark stains, like age spots.

'I wish they'd given us hazmat suits instead,' I said, trying to laugh off my disgust. Even with a discount, we'd obviously been ripped off.

'What do you mean?' She sounded defensive.

'Nothing.' I didn't want to offend her by criticising the place. The room she apparently loved.

When she pulled her top over her head, her ribcage jutted out under her skin. I grabbed my vestments and said I was going to the loo. We hadn't undressed in front of each other since getting changed for P.E. at school, and I was worried about her judging my body, the way it had thickened over the years.

I regretted my decision as soon as I opened the bathroom door. A musty smell hit me. The wooden toilet seat was split down the middle. The bathtub was ringed with dirt, the broken plug chain snaking along the bottom, next to a dead, curled-up spider. Around the windowsill, paint had puckered and lifted from the wall where mushrooms had pushed their way to the surface.

'Oh my god,' I shouted to Faith. 'There are mushrooms growing in here!'

No answer. Under my fingertip, the toadstools felt cold, fleshy.

While I hurriedly got changed, desperate to be out of this room, I looked through the window at the row of bins below, the round lid of a septic tank in the ground. My spirits sank.

In the bedroom, Faith was crouched next to her bed-side table, reaching into the narrow gap behind it. Her hand darted back as soon as she saw me come in.

'What are you doing?' I asked.

'Nothing. Switching on the plug socket.'

'Our bathroom has mushrooms.'

'It's the countryside. Things grow in the country-side. Relax and stop complaining.'

'I'm not complaining. It's just none of this is what I expected. Why didn't you tell me about the house rules? Signing the agreement?'

The words tumbled out before I could stop them. I waited for her anger to erupt.

Instead, her expression softened.

'Sorry, Luce. It completely slipped my mind with everything that's been going on. Mum, and everything.'

I felt a pang of guilt.

'You really don't need to worry, though,' she said. 'Trust me.'

That night, there was a Welcome Feast in honour of Esther and me, the newcomers. Everyone else had either been before, like Faith, or had stayed put for a long time.

A woman sitting next to me in the dining hall said she'd arrived six months ago. She'd only planned to stay a week.

'But as soon as I met Charles, I knew he could help me.'

Her name was Clover. She looked about forty, with rosy cheeks and a bob haircut.

'Before I came here, my M.E. was so bad I had to use a wheelchair. Look at me now!' She jumped to her feet and danced on the spot, before walking around the table to get more food.

After seeing the state of the room, I hadn't expected much from the buffet, but it was great. Bread rolls still warm from the oven. Roast beetroot and turnips and carrots, sweet and delicious. 'All grown onsite,' Karma told us. 'All organic, no chemicals or nasties.' Baked pike, which had been 'swimming in Murkwater this morning'.

'Nice surprise, isn't it,' said Esther, who caught my eye while I was piling vegetables onto my plate. 'Thought we'd have to survive on green tea.'

She was wearing grey vestments like everyone else, although she still had her sparkly pink glasses. Her matching walking stick was hooked onto the back of her chair. I told her I hadn't realised there was a dress code either.

'Charles said I'd be more comfortable in linen,' she said, 'but I drew a line when that woman asked me to hand over my glasses and cane. Cheeky bugger.'

I went back to my seat between Faith and Clover. It was hard to hear each other over chairs scraping across the floor as people got up to refill their plates, although Faith barely spoke. She was too busy shovelling food down. I hadn't seen her eat with this much relish since we were kids. Actually, I couldn't remember her eating anything on the two times we'd met up since reconnecting.

'So good, isn't it,' she said, her voice muffled by a mouthful of bread. 'Can't stand food anywhere else now. All the toxins.'

'Where's Charles? Isn't he coming?'

She laughed, her teeth and gums clagged with beige mush. 'No. He doesn't eat with us. He's got a private suite.'

We didn't see Charles the following day either. Karma led group yoga and meditation sessions. Faith and I sat in the outdoor sauna, a tiny cabin with windows looking out onto the woods, and watched deer grazing, pheasants strutting between the trees. It might have been peaceful, had Faith not jabbered on the whole time about Charles being a genius and ignored my attempts to change the subject.

In the cellar, there was a sensory deprivation tank, where I seized the opportunity for a few hours alone. As I lay in the tank, naked, floating on top of the salty water, staring into pitch black, strange shapes drifted into my vision. Rings of light. The dark had a fullness as though something else was there, hovering over me. Some unseen presence.

The next day, a rapping on our door woke us at dawn.

'Long day today, ladies,' said Karma behind the door. 'Get your skates on. Charles is waiting.'

In the entrance hall, people were scurrying to and fro with sandwiches and flasks, packing them into rucksacks. Charles strolled around, hands clasped behind his back, while everyone's eyes followed him around the room. No one explained anything properly, but I gathered we were going up Lyfell Pike.

'I can't,' I heard Esther saying to Karma, who she'd pulled to one side. 'My hip.'

Karma tutted at Esther like she was a difficult child. 'Now, that's a bit defeatist, isn't it? We mustn't let toxic thinking spoil things.'

'I'm not,' Esther insisted. 'I'm disabled.'

Karma pointed at a sweating, red-faced woman, who was hobbling to the door with a rucksack. 'Marie over there was told by some quack GP not to do anything strenuous because of her blood pressure, but she's not letting that stop her.'

'Maybe she should.'

'You can't miss mountain bathing! It'll sort that hip right out.'

'Look, I'm not going.'

Karma's smile evaporated, her voice dropped low.

'Well, someone will have to stay behind with you. They won't be able to go now either.'

She stormed off, leaving Esther on her own, staring down at her cane.

How was I going to manage? Going up a flight of stairs was often enough to trigger a flare-up. I was about to tell Esther I'd stay behind, too, when Faith returned with two pairs of walking boots, beaming at Charles as he walked past us.

She held out one of the pairs of boots. 'Size 6, right? These should fit. What's wrong?'

'I don't think I can do this. My cough.'

She put the boots down and took both my hands.

'You'll be fine. Promise. Once you're on the mountain...'

She trailed off and smiled, stroking my palms with her thumbs. It was a simple and gentle gesture, with the same ease and affection our physical contact always had when we were kids. Something I'd missed. Suddenly, I felt bad for feeling exasperated with her. She was trying to be a good friend. I didn't want to ruin it by not even attempting the hike.

Noah stayed behind with Esther while the rest of us set off. Everyone carried rucksacks except for Charles, who led the way, and Karma, who tailed at the back with Marie. We passed the glittering lake, a chicken coop, crows pecking in a wheatfield. A windowless wooden shack.

'Where they slaughter the chickens,' said Faith. 'Humanely, of course.'

My boots rubbed my feet, and blisters began to niggle my toes as we climbed the zigzag path around rocky ridges. Breathing grew heavier. Sweat dripped off faces. Soles slid on the scree, disturbing pebbles that rolled downhill. I hoisted the backpack up my aching shoulders, trying not to slip. The hall and grounds shrunk beneath us. Charles loomed above, not letting us stop for a break. His face was hidden in shadow as he called out over his shoulder, 'My favourite route, this. Great Heaven Gate.'

By the time we reached the summit, we were parched, searching in our rucksacks for flasks. When I tipped the contents into my mouth, I almost spat them back out. It wasn't water – it was bitter, vegetal. Some kind of herbal tea. I drank it, anyway, letting the liquid ease the dryness in my throat. Somehow, I'd made it up the mountain without coughing, but I didn't want to push it.

It was only then I took in the view. All around, between wisps of drifting cloud, the land undulated, dwarfed by the mountain we stood on. Woodland clung like moss around the foothills, while stubborn pockets of snow on summits refused to melt in the sun. The lake had become a shard of broken glass, a window to the perfect blue sky above.

Charles told us to gather around him in a circle.

'Isn't this glorious,' he said, smiling as he walked around, surveying each of us. 'This beautiful view proves what we already know. Nature is good for us. Nature heals. You know this instinctively. But you've been taught to ignore your instincts. You've cut your-selves off from them. And that's why you got sick.'

His eyes met mine, and my stomach flipped.

'With my help, you will recover that connection to nature. Recover yourself.'

He walked up to Faith. She closed her eyes as he rested his hand on her forehead.

'Accept Michael's blessing,' he said. 'Feel the mountain's energy flow through you.'

They stayed like that for a while, not moving. I scanned the other faces in the circle, trying to spot a raised eyebrow, a smirk. Surely no one was taking this seriously. But their expressions were solemn as they watched Charles and Faith, as though witnessing a ceremony. A baptism. A funeral.

Faith gasped.

Her eyelids fluttered as she arched her back, bending backwards further and further under Charles's hand, like a limbo dancer, before her knees buckled. She collapsed at his feet. On her back, she stretched out on the rocks, basking in his shadow and bursting into giddy laughter, the kind of hysterics she used to have when we were teenagers sneaking glasses of Merlot from my parents' wine box.

Charles turned to Marie next.

Marie had been the last one to reach the summit. When she finally made it, panting and drenched in sweat, she'd almost toppled headfirst into the cairn, before Karma caught her and gave her a flask. In the circle, she could barely stand, her weight seemingly held up by invisible strings – shoulders sagging, head drooping. As Charles approached her, she lifted her head slightly, a small brave smile on her red face.

The moment his hand touched her forehead, her whole body convulsed.

I almost rushed to her, thinking she was having a seizure. It was more like rapture – the expression on her face serene even as her arms shook violently at her sides. When Charles drew his hand away, she was a new woman, standing up straight, light on her feet, the redness in her skin faded to a healthy pink. She flashed us all a grin.

'I feel better,' she cried, 'so much better!'

I looked away and found Charles in front of me.

His palm was soft and warm on my forehead. I was embarrassed, more than anything. None of this could be real. These people were delusional. When absolutely nothing happened, they would think there was something wrong with me, not them. Should I fake a reaction, pretend to feel something?

No. I couldn't do it. I braced myself for dirty looks, whispers. Faith rallying the group against me.

Instead, a cool, liquid feeling trickled over me, like an egg cracked over my head. It coursed down my body. The raw feeling in my throat, aches in my shoulders, sharp swellings on my toes – all that pain melted away.

The last thing I saw before I sank to my knees was Charles's scarred lip curling into a smile.

On our way back to the house, Faith and I walked together, linking arms, both of us giggling as I tried and failed to express what I'd just experienced.

'I know,' she said. 'Isn't it amazing?'

I looked behind me a few times to take in the view. Marie was lagging behind again. She wasn't smiling anymore, and she kept stopping to catch her breath, clutching her chest. Karma was at her side, speaking to her, but I couldn't hear what she said.

During our free hour before dinner, Faith suggested heading to the library. I was tired in a comfortable, satisfied way from the hike, dazed from whatever had happened on the mountain, so the idea of curling up with a book sounded nice.

A few other guests were in the library, reading or napping on the sofa beside a crackling log fire. Noah sat in the corner, a book open on his lap. He was watching us, smiling. Wherever we went in the house, aside from our room, there was always at least one staff member around in case we needed anything.

We browsed the bookshelves. Faith had said there was an amazing selection, but it was mostly books by Charles Hartman, along with some spiritual and self-help stuff, a few Lake District guidebooks in faded print. It only took her a few seconds to choose something – a fantasy novel judging by the strange winged creature on the cover and the title, *Spirit of the Mountain*. Also by Charles. I picked up another copy and skimmed the blurb before putting it back, although, weeks later, I'd read the full thing. It's about a group of refugees from a toxic wasteland who hide up a mountain. One of them, Charles, has special powers. He's visited by a great spirit called Michael, who allows the group to stay in exchange for love. They live happily and peacefully, until one of the women rejects Charles's and Michael's love. She's banished forever, doomed to a horrible death in the wasteland.

When I first picked it up, I thought it was fiction.

Copies of *Toxic People* filled an entire shelf. Other guests had been raving about this book at s, and I'd felt left out, having only read a couple of paragraphs of the copy Faith had given me, although Esther confessed she hadn't read it either. It deserved another chance. Mountain bathing was nothing like I'd ever experienced – I wanted to know how this 'process' worked.

A copy tucked at the end of the shelf caught my eye. The dust jacket was a fainter shade of red than the rest, scuffed and torn at the edges. I pulled it off the shelf and sat on a wingback chair near Faith, who was already engrossed in her book.

I opened the book carefully, trying to make sure the cover didn't fall apart. The margins on every page were covered in notes and symbols in blue ink. Entire paragraphs had been underlined, with exclamation marks and asterisks marked next to them. The book had been pored over so many times, some of its pages were coming apart from the spine.

On the inside cover, it said:

`property of j.b.`

Transcript Excerpt #3

ME: Sorry, did you say their initials were "J.B."?
LUCY: Yeah.
ME: Give me a minute.

> *[I get up and rush out of the room, leaving my empty chair and thrown-open study door on my webcam view. Lucy gazes out from her screen, eyes narrowed, looking confused. I reappear through the study door carrying a document and take my seat.]*

ME: Did the handwriting look like this?

> *[I hold up the unfolded page of a letter, handwritten in blue ink, signed by Julie. I move it closer to my camera: the words blur on my screen. Lucy squints.]*

LUCY: I can't see properly – can you hold it back a bit?

[I move the letter back slightly, where it comes into clearer focus.]

ME: Well? Does it look the same?

LUCY: It could be. I'm not certain.

ME: Try to remember.

JULIE: I am trying, Richard.

ME: Sorry. It's just it would be good to verify if it was hers. Do you still have that copy of the book?

LUCY: Not anymore.

ME: *[sighs]* Right, right. Tell me what else you remember about it, then.

Lucy

J.B. HAD DRAWN LITTLE blue hearts around the opening sentence.

Modernisation is the opium of the people, and the people are sickening.

The first bit of the introduction is about how industrialisation and urbanisation alienated man from the means of his own creation – nature. *Without proximity to natural beauty, man wilts like a flower in shade.* Rapid technological advances are making this worse.

Man has become a thoroughly domesticated animal, born into captivity, spending his life in cages.

I pondered over this sentence for a while, thinking about my own life. How I was thoroughly institutionalised. A blue biro arrow pointed from the word *cages* to a scribbled list:

```
home
school
work
hospital
nursing home
```

I read on. *Modernity offers comfort and convenience as guards against unpredictable nature.* Supposedly to improve health and quality of life. In reality, modern society exposes us to airborne pollutants, synthetic chemicals, unnatural radiation levels – all poisoning and prematurely ageing the body. This is why rates of cancer, autoimmune disorders, and infertility are increasing in young people. A blue circle around *infertility*.

Charles wrote that back in the late 70s, but it could have been written today. I'd read articles about rises in early-onset cancer and autoimmune disease.

The good news is the damage can be undone. With nature exposure therapy – close contact with places of outstanding natural beauty – and guidance from an expert healer, people detoxify, and health and youth can be restored. But there's a warning.

The toxicity of modern life is so invasive, it infects us neurologically, changing how we think.

Neurological toxicity is pernicious. Most people aren't aware they have it. It's a form of dementia, tricking its host into believing they're thinking and behaving rationally.

Thankfully, neurological toxicity can be reversed with nature exposure therapy, but the individual has to work hard to undo residual toxic thinking, such as refusing to accept an expert healer's diagnosis or treatment. Or remaining attached to their harmful lifestyle. Or being unwilling to cut ties with toxic people. Next to this phrase, another note in the margin:

`mum` and `dad`

If illness isn't cured with nature exposure therapy, the reason is persistent toxic thinking. We can only fully heal by purging neurological toxicity entirely. It's a long, difficult process.

Purging may mimic symptoms of disease, leading some patients to mistakenly assume the therapeutic process itself is making them sick.

Because of this, people often abandon treatment too soon and blame natural healing for making their illnesses worse. Again, this is toxic thinking, all too common in those who defer to modern medicine despite its harmful methods.

The next sentence was underlined three times. My heart skipped a beat as I read it.

Perhaps the apotheosis of neurological toxicity takes place in the chemotherapy unit, where nurses counter-intuitively administer toxic chemicals to treat illness, performing a delusional duty of care.

Memories flooded back of patients coming through the hospice doors, held up by their exhausted-looking partners or adult children, or wheeled in if they were no longer strong enough to walk. Many of them had undergone chemo, hoping it might save them.

Like them, I'd trusted medicine.

Under that sentence, J.B. had written:

`i've been wrong about everything`

The dinner bell rang, and Noah started ushering everyone out of the library.

I held up the book. 'Is it okay if I borrow this?'

He snatched it from my hands, flipped through the pages.

'It was like that when I opened it,' I said, not wanting him to think I'd written all over it.

He closed the book and turned it over, frowning as he surveyed the back cover.

'First edition, this. Bit worse for wear. People shouldn't deface books, especially Charles's books.' He pointed to the bookshelf. 'We've got plenty of copies.'

'I don't mind. I like first editions.'

The truth was the notes intrigued me as much as the book itself. I worried he'd confiscate it, but he gave it back and nudged me out the door.

In the dining hall, I didn't taste the food on my plate, didn't realise what I was eating. Thoughts flurried through my mind. The mountaintop. Charles's hand on my forehead. That cracked-egg anaesthetic sensation. Phrases from *Toxic People* came back to me on a loop, like melodies from catchy songs.

Esther clicked her fingers. 'Earth to Lucy. I've said your name, like, five times. Are you okay? Why's everyone so out of it?'

I became aware of the steady scraping of cutlery on plates – muffled, as though I was underwater. Esther's voice was the only clear sound.

'Long day.' I was tired and wanted dinner to be over so I could read more *Toxic People*.

Esther leaned closer, lowered her voice. 'How was mountain bathing?'

'Weird. Incredible.'

'Oh, god. Don't tell me you've joined the Charles Hartman Fan Club. I need an ally in here.' She glanced around the table. 'Where's Marie?'

I looked left and right, scanning the now-familiar faces. Marie wasn't there.

A chair scraped across the floor, and a bell-like sound rang from the head of the table. Karma was on her feet, tapping her glass with a spoon. Everyone else fell silent.

'Excuse me, darlings. I have an announcement.'

Esther piped up. 'Is it about Marie? Where's she gone?'

Karma's smile flickered at the interruption.

'Marie had to leave, I'm afraid. But I have good news. Charles will be doing personal consultations tomorrow. Isn't that wonderful! I've drawn up a rota so you'll all get a slot.'

As she sat down, the room swarmed with excited babble, everyone suddenly animated, repeating the words 'Charles' and 'tomorrow'.

Faith let out a sigh. 'Finally.'

She squeezed my hand under the table, her eyes bright in the candlelight.

In our room, she fell asleep within minutes. Even though I was exhausted, I stayed up to read the next chapter of *Toxic People*, about nature exposure therapy and how it's most effective on mountains.

Mountains are the pinnacle of natural beauty, hence their significance in religious and canonical literature.

This chapter has gorgeous illustrations of Mount Olympus, Sinai, Athos, Purgatory. *Souls purge their sins to ascend Mount Purgatory and reach the Earthly Paradise at the summit.* J.B. noted in the margin: purge toxic thoughts to heal.

There are black-and-white photos of Cumbrian mountains – Helvellyn, Great Gable, Blencathra. Lyfell Pike takes up a full page. Below the picture, J.B. had scrawled:

`don't leave`

My consultation was mid-afternoon, just before Faith's. When the time came, I gripped the banister as I went upstairs, trying to control the trembling in my legs. Passing the first floor where the guests' rooms were, I went up to the second floor as Karma had instructed. The second floor was off-limits to guests.

At the end of a long corridor, I found Charles's private suite, his name in gold lettering on the door. My hand shook as I knocked. I told myself not to expect too much. Charles would tell me there was nothing wrong with me, nothing he could do to help, like all the doctors I'd seen.

A voice behind the door.

'Come in.'

Thin net curtains veiled the windows, giving the room a soft, dreamy light. As I closed the door, smells of sandalwood and leather and musty old books rose to meet me. On my left was an examination table and a foldable privacy screen. On my right, a desk laid with bronze measuring scales, a pestle and mortar, jars of herbs and spices. Smoke rising from a joss stick. Along the walls, between overstuffed bookshelves, hung paintings of Lyfell Pike, anatomical drawings. One showed a corpse lying on the anatomist's table, smiling placidly, pulling open his own skin.

Charles was sitting near the fireplace, one leg crossed over the other. I sank into the soft leather armchair opposite and immediately felt sleepy – the air was warm and close. Behind his horn-rimmed glasses, Charles's eyes were deep blue.

He asked how was I feeling today, had I enjoyed my stay so far, what brought me to the retreat. He seemed genuinely curious, relaxed, in no rush at all, even though I knew he had other consultations after mine. Each time I finished speaking, he left long pauses, waiting for me to say more.

I told him about my chronic cough, how no one had been able to work out what caused it.

He nodded, stroking his beard. 'Any flare-ups over the past few days?'

'Actually, no.' This had already occurred to me while I'd been waiting for my consultation and planning what I'd say.

I hadn't had a coughing fit since coming to the retreat.

'But it comes and goes,' I said, wanting him to know I was still concerned. 'Things trigger it, like stress.'

When I'd mentioned this to doctors, they'd recommended finding ways to manage stress – mindfulness, and so on. It used to piss me off. Stress isn't always manageable, is it? Sometimes life is brutal. My parents dying. Splitting up with Nate. Stress was routine in my line of work. I couldn't abandon patients lying in their own shit to go off and do some meditation.

I never said any of this out loud, of course. I'm a health professional, too. I've given similar well-meaning advice to my own patients, dozens, hundreds of times.

I was certain Charles was about to give tips on managing stress. He said nothing for a while, watching me, making sure I'd finished.

'Mind if I take a look?' He gestured towards the examination table.

Even though I've examined countless patients in my career, I hate being examined. Having to undress behind a curtain and call when you're ready, with nothing but a flimsy sheet of paper to preserve your dignity. Staring up at the ceiling, at the fluorescent strip lighting – anything but the examiner's face. The snap of rubber gloves. The chill of metal instruments on bare flesh. The humiliation of insertion.

This wasn't like any medical examination I'd had before.

Charles didn't make me undress. Not that time. I lay down, fully clothed, bracing myself for whatever was about to happen. He moved to the end of the table and closed his eyes, suspending his hands above my toes, as though there was a force field around me. Slowly, his hands drifted over my shins, thighs, pelvis – he paused here, frowning – then carried on over my torso, pausing again at my throat. When he reached my head, he stopped and opened his eyes.

'You're doing great, Lucy. I'll go over once again to make sure I haven't missed anything.'

Starting again at my feet, his hands hovered over my body, pausing halfway. I flinched when they touched my hips, like two small birds simply landing there, taking rest. He frowned again, while I told myself to relax. Surely this was routine, nothing to worry about.

His hands took flight and glided an inch over my belly, my chest, my collarbone, falling onto my neck. His thumbs pressed my throat.

When he was done, he invited me to sit with him by the fire. He scribbled on a notepad, crossed something out, made another note. Then he looked up, his expression solemn.

'I'm sorry to tell you this, Lucy. But you are gravely ill.'

I let his words sink in. Rather than panicking, I felt strangely soothed. Finally, someone believed me. Unlike the doctors who'd hustled me out of their offices, thinking I was a timewaster, a hypochondriac.

He leaned forward and traced the tip of his index finger down my neck. 'I felt it here straight away. Hardened oesophagus, an obstruction. Most likely a malignant tumour.' He cocked his head to one side. 'Let me guess. Doctors didn't find anything.'

'But I had all these tests.'

He shook his head, his scarred lip twisting into a cynic's smile. He'd heard this before.

'It's not your fault. Doctors act like those tests are gospel, but they yield limited data. They miss subtle but important signs. Only a skilled Healer would detect them.'

'What signs?' I asked. 'What type of cancer is it? What stage?'

He shook his head and smiled. 'Is that really what you want? To be reduced to a tissue name and a numeral?'

He explained how holistic medicine considers the whole individual, looks for emotional and spiritual signs as much as physical ones. 'The location of the primary tumour isn't random. Areas of the body with deep emotional associations are more vulnerable to disease. Doctors don't understand that. They are emotionally illiterate.'

I'd like to think I didn't accept what he told me right away, that I challenged him. The truth is he barely had to parry my questions. The rational part of my brain was backing into a corner, cowed by his assertiveness, his superior knowledge.

'What should I do?' I asked, finally.

He flicked back through his notepad and nodded at something he saw there. 'You said you haven't had any flare-ups since you arrived. Good. The therapy's already working.'

'I'm going home in a couple of days.'

He glanced at me over the top of his glasses with something like pity.

'I don't think that's a good idea. Do you?'

'I don't know.' My voice cracked, mouth suddenly dry. 'It's a lot of money.'

'Nothing's more valuable than health.'

He put down his notepad and sat back in his chair, his fingertips together, forming a steeple.

'Obviously, it's up to you,' he said. 'I just worry what will happen if you leave.'

The tumour had metastasised, he explained. It was in my lungs, causing my breathing problems. It was elsewhere, too.

'I noticed something wasn't right in your pelvic area. Though I'd have to do another examination to be sure.'

'Can you get rid of them? The tumours?'

'Certainly. I must warn you, though, you've got a long road ahead. It's going to take time and commitment. The treatment's starting to take effect, as you know.'

That's why I'd felt better since arriving here. Stronger. Energetic. I breathed easily.

He mentioned scream therapy, one of the activities offered at the retreat. 'In my experience, this is a very effective complementary therapy for diseases of the throat. It may prove difficult or even impossible for you at first but keep going with it.'

'How long do you think I should stay?'

'Everyone's different. Some take weeks, others years.'

'I have to go back to work. If they don't sack me first. I've already been off sick for months.'

He flipped through his notes. 'A palliative care nurse. You want to go back?'

'I need a job.'

'Does it have to be that job?'

I had to think about it. Whether I could face nursing again. The bittersweet joy of getting to know my patients, their families and histories, building rapport and trust with them while watching them decline. The stab in the gut when they pass away.

'You've got what it takes to be a great Healer,' he said. 'I'd personally supervise your training.'

He warned me I'd be wasting my talents if I went back, not to mention ruining my health. He'd seen it happen many times over the years.

'A young nurse came here a while back. She was like you. Special. So much potential. She could have made a real difference, had she become a Healer. But she gave in to toxic thinking and left too soon, and it killed her. A tragic loss.'

By the time I came out of my consultation, it was getting dark. I found Karma and told her about the arrangements I'd discussed with Charles, to extend my stay at least another month and see how I went on.

'No problem, angel,' she said. 'I'll get that all sorted for you.'

There was no discount this time. I gave her my bank details anyway. If Charles was right, if I was riddled with tumours, it would be madness to leave now. The retreat was the only thing helping me feel better. It was worth the money.

I didn't see Faith until dinner, when she slumped into the chair next to me. She poked at her salad.

'How was it?' I asked.

She glared at me. 'You shouldn't ask. It's confidential.'

I said I was sorry and she shrugged, tearing up her salad leaves with her fingers. Something besides my faux pas was bothering her. She'd probably bite my head off if I asked what.

I told her about extending my stay. 'Charles found tumours, even though all those doctors missed them. But I've not been coughing since we arrived. This place is working, like you said it would.'

She snorted. 'Yeah. Works wonders.' I wondered what she meant, why her tone was off, but she she'd extended her stay, too.

I couldn't stop myself. 'Get this. Charles said he'd train me to be a Healer. Because I'm special, apparently.' I laughed it off, even though I'd felt genuinely flattered at Charles's offer.

Faith dropped her shredded leaves and looked at me.

'He said that?'

'Yeah. Ridiculous, right?'

'That is ridiculous. Liar.'

A jolt, like she'd slapped me in the face. 'What?'

She pushed her plate away. 'You're lying. He never said that to you.'

'Why are you being like this? What's the matter with you?'

'You wouldn't even be here if it wasn't for me.' We sat in silence. I couldn't eat anymore. I was shivering, my teeth chattering. How could she accuse me of lying? It was so unfair. Then again, it was my fault she didn't trust a word I said, wasn't it? After the way I'd treated her in Sixth Form. Guilt twisted a knot in my stomach. The feverish anger coursing through my body had nowhere else to go, so I sealed it away a tight pocket, hidden, like the tumour in my neck.

The servers came round to clear the table. Usually, we took this as our cue to leave the dining hall, but Faith stayed behind, piling her plate on top of mine and carrying them to the kitchen. Why? To avoid me? Play the martyr?

I went straight up to our room, too wound up to join the other guests in the entrance hall, where we usually drifted after dinner to sit and chat. As soon as I got in bed, I picked up *Toxic People* and looked up throat disease in the index. It's mentioned in a chapter on complementary therapies alongside nature exposure therapy, including scream therapy. *Screaming reduces toxic concentrations in the body, especially in the throat, where disease susceptibility is increased by inhibited self-expression and issues of communication.*

I squinted at a note cramped into the top of the page.

```
toxic habits eat your body, un-
dermining recovery. your toxicity
harms everyone, spawning illness.
charles knows only nature ends suf-
fering.
```

The blue ink faded out in places, like J.B.'s pen had been drying up when they wrote it. The wavering letters looked manic.

Faith came in, and I closed the book. She'd noticed me poring over it the day before and had asked why I didn't swap it for a nice, clean copy. I didn't feel like explaining why I'd held onto it, how I was enjoying getting to know this previous guest, whoever they were. Making a new friend.

Then I remembered Faith and I weren't on speaking terms. She caught my eye, a sheepish look on her face.

'Sorry for being a bitch earlier,' she said.

'It's okay. Don't worry about it. Where've you been?'

She fell onto her bed, kicked her shoes off. 'Washing up.'

'Why?'

'Money's tight, so they're letting me do some voluntary work instead of paying. So, I can stay longer.'

'How much longer? Aren't you cured?'

She rubbed her eyes. 'When I went home, I went against Charles's recommendation. He said the tumour was gone, but there could still be traces. But I wanted to see Mum and talk her into coming. Plus, I was running out of money. I only went home for a few months. I thought I'd be alright.' Her voice broke as she started to cry. 'But I'm not. It's relapsed. Charles said it's more aggressive than before. I've got to stay until it's completely gone, and who knows how long that'll take.' She shook her head, let out a hollow laugh. 'He said he'd train me to be a Healer, actually, when I came last time. He didn't say anything about that today. So, it looks like I've fucked that one up.'

I went to her side, tried to comfort her. 'You can't volunteer while you're ill. There must be another way.'

'There isn't. Anyway, Charles says volunteering helps you heal. Giving something back breaks selfish, toxic patterns.'

She had to get up early for breakfast duty, so we tried to get some sleep. I dreamt about being on the mountain, something gliding towards me. It was so bright, I couldn't see what it was, even when I felt its hands on my face.

I woke with a start. Stared at the pale strip of moonlight around the edge of the curtains, the crack across the ceiling. It was windy outside, and the window kept creaking, the roof shingles rattling.

I wanted to switch on the light to read, but I was worried about disturbing Faith. She needed rest. She was lying on her back, a pool of light on her throat, smooth skin concealing alien growths beneath. I pressed my fingers against my own throat, unable to feel the lump Charles had found. Then again, I wasn't an expert Healer with thirty years' experience. Perhaps I could be in the future – Charles saw my potential. Only, it bothered me slightly that he'd said the same thing to Faith.

I rolled onto my other side and gazed at *Toxic People* on my bedside table. The blurb was unreadable in the darkness, but I could make out the ghostly shape of Charles's face, his aviator glasses and almost-smile. In the photo, his lips were smooth.

Between then and now, how did he get that scar?

Hell's Healer:

a short biography of Charles Hartman

ACCORDING TO THE HART Company website, Charles Hartman is a 'celebrated' author who has 'practiced natural healing for over thirty-five years'. His first book, *Toxic People*, published in 1978, was an 'instant international bestseller', with more than two million copies sold worldwide.

Since then, Hartman published twenty more books, though none enjoyed the success of his debut, as their barest mention on the Hart website seems to attest. This includes his 1984 utopian novel, *Spirit of the Mountain*, and his 1990 memoir, *Blessed*. In the latter's preface, Hartman explains his motivation for writing an autobiography.

I was tired of copycats falsely claiming to be Healers and luring gullible people into their midst. Few are truly blessed with the power to heal, having been specially chosen by divine beings who reside on mountaintops.

Hartman's arrogance is perhaps most outrageously on display in the biblical rhetoric of *Blessed,* as this choice paragraph demonstrates:

On the sixth day, I reached the summit of Lyfell Pike, where I was visited by the great spirit Michael.

And unto me, Michael said, 'Behold! You shall be transformed into my conduit on earth, delivering my blessing of health to all who are worthy.

Unsurprisingly, *Blessed* was a commercial failure.

However, poor sales of his later books hardly mattered. *Toxic People* set Hartman's legacy in stone and would attract fans to his Cumbrian retreat for decades to come.

Prior to publishing *Toxic People,* Hartman began his career as a 'top student' – his website's words, not mine – of medicine at a renowned London university (incidentally, where I began my degree in 1972, a year after Charles began his), before he dropped out. I was intrigued as to why.

I tracked down Professor Arthur Appleby, who taught at the university's Faculty of Medicine from 1959 until he retired in 1994. I explained I was a former student of his medical history and ethics class – who he may recall always sat on the second-to-left front row seat of the lecture theatre and took copious notes – and was currently writing a book about another erstwhile student of his, Charles Hartman. Alas, the good professor did not remember me; he did, however, remember Hartman.

'The one who wrote that book?' His wavering voice had, sadly, lost its sonority with age. 'He was a queer one. Interested in miracle cures, supposed resurrections, that sort of nonsense. Instead of handing in an essay on, say, the impact of John Snow's cholera studies, he'd submit some rambling hypothesis on achieving immortality.'

The professor sighed deeply before he went on.

'He simply did not have the correct mindset for medicine. A mind dulled by fairy stories and old wives' tales. He did hail from a backward sort of place. Some miserable northern town. Bolton or Blackburn or Burnley.'

When I casually commented that I also came from a northern town, the professor hastened to retract his aspersions of the North: 'I trained some very fine doctors from the North, very fine indeed.'

After ending my conversation with the professor, I followed this geographical lead to search for details of Hartman's childhood, about which there is no information on his website or in any of his printed works. Luckily for me, Hartman is not a common name in Lancashire: without too much difficulty, I located the birth certificate of a Charles Hartman in Blackburn in 1953. Using this record, I traced the nearest branches of his family tree.

His mother, Bethan, began her training as a Staff Nurse at the Blackburn Royal Infirmary in 1948, the year the NHS was established, before becoming a midwife. At that time, there was a general mistrust of hospitals among expectant mothers in the local community, with many opting to give birth at home. Bethan's services would have been called upon at any time, day or night, sometimes for many hours, especially if there were complications. Her days would have been long, especially after her husband, Charles, became ill. Before his convalescence, he had been employed as a maintenance worker in a mill that used asbestos. He died at home in 1960, aged forty-two.

Bethan was left with four children to raise on her own: Margaret, who'd just turned fourteen; Caroline, aged ten; Charles, aged seven; and Emma, the baby of the family, who was not yet two. Margaret likely took up duties at home while her mother was at work, cooking and cleaning and looking after the younger children, probably grudgingly at a time when youth culture and second-wave feminism were gaining momentum.

Meanwhile, bereavement and hard work must have taken their toll on Bethan. On the 21st of October 1962, the *Blackburn Times* reported the return of a famous clairvoyant, Donna Taylor, to the Blackburn Spiritualist Church. Bethan Hartman is quoted in the article: 'Donna helped me communicate with my late husband when she came last year. I was going through a very difficult time, but connecting to the spirit world brought me closure. Her readings and guidance are helping me heal.' Unless Bethan left her children at home while going to church, they likely joined her for these services. One wonders what young Charles might have felt witnessing séances. Fear? Awe? Fascination?

In 1963, tragedy struck the family once again. Emma Hartman's death certificate states she accidentally drowned in the bath at home. The official records do not tell us who bore responsibility. Was it Margaret, reluctantly tasked with bathing her youngest sister and negligent in her care? Or was it the fault of her inattentive, grief-befuddled mother? Had one of the other children engaged their sister in rough play that went wrong?

After Emma's death, Charles did not remain in the Hartman residence for long. Census data shows him living with his great uncle, Isaac Porter, in Cumbria in 1966, before he enrolled at a single-sex boarding school in Patterdale. He must have excelled academically if his uncle was prepared to foot the bill for his private education; the fees were beyond what his mother could afford. Was this the sole reason why the boy was sent away so soon after his sister's death – to improve his future prospects? Or did grave concerns impel Bethan to dispatch her son: an inability to cope with a troublesome boy, perhaps? Concern for her surviving daughters: a mother's protective instincts?

Whatever the basis for Charles's move to Cumbria, it would turn out to be the making of him.

During his time at university, Hartman grew disillusioned with 'the flaws of modern medicine', as his company's website puts it. In 1974, aged twenty-one, he 'abandoned' – or, perhaps, if we read between the lines, failed – his studies and left London to travel the world.

Hartman writes of his jaunt across South Asia in *Blessed*, detailing preposterous anecdotes: how he helped a seventy-year-old woman give birth to a healthy baby boy; cured a community of lepers; enabled a paraplegic child to recover the use of her limbs. But illness was unrelenting. It always returned. He dreamed of a beautiful place where the sick would be permanently cured. Where nothing besides insufficient willpower stood in the way of perfect health.

His enlightenment, as he calls it, took place not in the ashrams of South Asia, but Cumbria, where he returned in 1976. He lived a peripatetic life, moving between campsites and youth hostels across the county as he penned early drafts of *Toxic People*. It was the summit of Lyfell Pike where, Hartman wrote, he found his faith in the sublime beauty of nature. Or was it rather where he discovered the idea to reinvent himself as God? From the mountaintop he looked down upon all he wished to possess: the youth hostel where he'd spent the night; the valley of Blundale stretching out below, its lake and woods and meadows; the lost souls drawn here, seeking salvation. All this would be his Eden.

The youth hostel closed down; the building reopened as the Hartman Health Centre.

If there is scant information about Hartman's background, there is even less about his inner circle: those who have resided at the retreat and served on its staff since its early years. His closest aide, known only as Karma, came to the retreat shortly after it opened. An old Hartman Health Centre brochure from 1979, which I came across in 's archives, includes a photograph of a woman painting an enormous portrait of Hartman on a piece of fabric. She cannot be more than eighteen years old. Another photo shows her sat on a grassy hill in Lotus Pose. Below, the caption reads: *Karma, our resident yogi, will help you connect your mind, body and spirit.* She wears a crown of daisies on top of her waist-length, blonde hair; the camera has caught her in mid-laughter.

In another brochure from 1984, she is pictured again: her head is shaved. Her cheeks are hollow. She no longer smiles. Her eyes are closed, as though she is in deep meditation, and the rest of the world is shut out.

Lucy

OUR MEALS SHRANK. A bowl of porridge became a spoonful. Soup came without bread. Fish and chicken disappeared from our plates, replaced with smatterings of cabbage.

By this point, I'd got to the chapter on diet in *Toxic People*, how food grown organically in places of outstanding natural beauty is pure, whereas food produced elsewhere is toxic. The best way to detoxify the body was to not eat, or eat less, and let the toxins clear out from your digestive system. Fasting optimised your health, helped you ascend to a higher state of consciousness. *Medieval saints communed with Christ through fasting.*

Whenever I felt dizzy from hunger, I thought about the good I was doing my body, about J.B.'s note in the margin:

```
impure food cravings = toxic
thinking
```

There were no clocks or calendars in the house, and I lost track of how many days had passed since we'd arrived. Hours filled with supervised group activities, the rumble of empty stomachs. Karma led art therapy sessions. We weaved baskets, made candles, painted pictures of Lyfell Pike. Charles chose the best paintings for displaying on the walls. We filled neck pouches with lavender and chamomile to ward away toxicity and induce calm. We did yoga and meditation and mountain bathing. We were so busy, there was barely chance to think. It was easier that way. Making simple decisions had become difficult, like which direction to take to get to the dining hall or the drawing room – I'd see other guests hesitate at the bottom of the stairs.

My thoughts only defogged while reading *Toxic People,* when I saw things with a new clarity, like wearing glasses for the first time.

Faith served dinner before joining us at the table. She hunched over as she ate, not joining in the conversations around her. In addition to getting up early for breakfast duty, she was now helping to cook and serve dinner, as well as washing up and cleaning the kitchen afterwards. Dark circles ringed her eyes.

Esther frowned at the tiny portion of salad Faith had put down in front of her. Following her consultation with Charles, she'd also extended her stay. 'He's a lovely man,' she'd told me. 'He really got me, what I'd gone through. Said there was loads he could do for the pain. Nice change from doctors giving me steroid injections that don't work or basically telling me to suck it up.'

After her consultation, her attitude changed. She stopped rolling her eyes at meditation and art therapy. She listened intently when the group discussed *Tox-*

ic People. Earlier that day, rather than staying behind while everyone else went mountain bathing, she said she'd come along. People cheered, and she even got an approving smile from Karma.

It didn't last long.

Esther hobbled up the narrow footpath as long as she could before she stopped, leaning on her cane, saying it was too much for her. Charles tried to persuade her to carry on, but she insisted on going back. Noah assisted Esther down the slope, while Charles led the rest of us uphill, delivering a sermon on willpower being key to healing.

When we got back, she looked deflated and hurt, wincing as she dropped to her seat in the dining hall. Her bright pink nail polish had chipped. When she finished her salad, she called to Faith. 'Is there any more of this?'

Faith looked up, blankly. 'That's the allowance.'

Karma was doing her nightly round of the dining table, checking in with each of the guests. Esther waved her over. 'Excuse me, can I have more to eat, please? I'm still hungry.'

Karma smirked. 'More? That would exceed your diet plan.'

'I'm not on a diet.'

Karma continued to smile. 'But you are, pet. You agreed to all aspects of the therapy, including the diet plan, when you signed the agreement.'

'This is ridiculous. The rates you charge, we should get a decent meal.'

Esther's voice rang out in the room. Everyone looked over.

Karma bent down to Esther's ear, her voice low. 'Let's chat about this another time. Privately. Rather than distracting other guests with your toxic energy while they're trying to heal.'

I waited for Esther to retaliate, but she went quiet and kept her head down after that, busying herself with wiping her glasses on the corner of her tunic. I felt bad for her, although I sided with Karma. We had a diet plan for a good reason.

Still, I didn't like the way Karma had spoken to her.

The next morning, Karma led us into the woods for scream therapy.

It had rained overnight, so the path was slippery. Esther's cane kept sliding around and getting stuck in the mud, and she lagged behind.

Karma did not stop or slow down.

There had been no newcomers at the retreat since Esther and me, but a few returning guests arrived. One was Dan. He recognised Faith from his previous stay and hugged her, asking how she'd been, when she got back.

'I'm staying for good this time,' he said. 'Are you?'

'How come you left?' she asked.

'I had some things to take care of. Quitting my job, signing divorce papers. I've been busy!'

The air stank of wild garlic. A couple of staff members were kneeling down on the ground, gathering ribbony green leaves and star-shaped white flowers into baskets.

Dan asked if I was looking forward to scream therapy. I told him Charles had recommended it in my consultation.

'Well, Charles knows best,' Dan said. 'Only, some people don't get him. Closed-minded types. My wife – ex-wife – hated it here...'

'Why?'

'She got angry when Charles told me to stop taking lithium. But I'm so glad I did. I felt like myself for the first time in years. A real man. Not some zombie, with all that toxic shit in my brain. Anyway, she kept complaining until she got her way and we went home. Then she tried to force me back on meds and stop me coming back. I said to her, "How do you expect me to be a good husband? A good father?' We've got two kids, see. But she wouldn't listen."'

I was wrapping my head around the fact he wasn't planning to go back to his kids when he asked how many times I'd read *Toxic People*.

'It's my first time,' I said.

'I'm so jealous. Wish I could experience that again. Waking up from the Matrix.'

We stopped in a clearing where bright green moss coated the ground, rocks, fallen trees, absorbing the sound of our footsteps.

Karma turned to face us.

'We'll make a start shortly,' she said. 'First, a question for our lovely newcomers. When was the last time you screamed?'

Everyone looked at me and Esther.

Esther shrugged. 'Not since I was a kid. I'm a teacher, so I've often felt like it.'

Karma nodded. 'And why do we scream as children?'

I remembered a passage from *Toxic People* that J.B. had underlined.

'We scream to survive,' I said. 'Babies scream for food, attention.'

Karma beamed. 'That's right, my love. Someone's done their homework. Screaming is an instinct we're born with but taught to repress. Scream therapy reconnects us with our natural instincts. With nature itself.'

We spread out, each finding our own spot in the clearing. Karma instructed us to focus on a strong emotion and let it out.

There were about ten of us in the group, all watching each other, waiting for someone else to go first.

What the hell was I doing here?

Then came the first scream.

It was Dan, wailing, curtains of blonde hair quivering over his eyes. A strand of spit dangling from his lips. Behind him, Esther looked shocked, one hand grasping her cane, the other pressed over her mouth.

Other guests joined in with Dan. Clover dropped to her knees and grabbed fistfuls of moss, flinging them in the air as she cried out.

I tried to shake off my awkwardness and have a go. The first emotion that came to me was anger – at getting ill, at my body betraying me. I focused on it, like Karma said. Opened my mouth.

No sound came out.

I massaged my throat, swallowed a few times, tried to force out even just a noisy breath.

Nothing.

Karma was watching me closely, as though she knew Charles had said I'd find scream therapy difficult. I dismissed the idea. Charles wouldn't have told her. Our consultations were confidential.

My thoughts were interrupted by an awful screech behind me.

A dying animal.

I wheeled around. Faith was kneeling in the mud, screaming. Punching herself. Scratching her face.

I ran to her side and grabbed her hands, forcing them away from her cheeks, which were covered in red, raw marks, so deep she'd drawn blood.

'It's my fault. All my fault,' she sobbed, over and over.

My voice came back as I begged her to stop, to tell me what was wrong.

'I'm disgusting. Toxic. I deserve fucking cancer.'

Then she fell silent. Her whole body went limp, her head flopping onto my shoulder as I caught her.

That's when I noticed everyone else had stopped screaming. They'd circled around us, watching Faith with repulsed curiosity. A freakshow.

Only Esther stepped forward, concerned, balancing on her cane as she eased down beside us.

'She's passed out,' I said.

Esther turned to the others. 'Someone call an ambulance!'

'Hush, hush,' said Karma. 'No need for a fuss.' She bent down and pinched Faith's chin, twisting her head left, then right. Faith flinched at her touch.

Karma stood up again. 'She's absolutely fine. She just connected with some strong emotions. Only, poor thing overlooked an important distinction between releasing emotions and wallowing in them. One's natural and healthy. The other...'

Faith didn't look fine. Blood was smeared on her cheeks, under her nails. She was pale and clammy, like she was about to be sick.

I looked up at Karma. 'She's really ill.'

Faith shrugged off my arm.

'Leave it, Luce,' she mumbled, slowly getting to her feet. I offered my hand to help her up, which she ignored.

Karma asked Dan to lead the rest of the group back to the house. 'I'll stay with Faith, make sure she's okay.'

Faith stared at her feet, silent.

'Are you sure?' I said, more to Faith, but Karma shooed me away. I had a bad feeling about leaving Faith after seeing Karma lash out at Esther. For all Karma's kindliness and positivity, she had a mean side. A bullying streak.

I looked back over my shoulder, saw Karma whispering in Faith's ear. Dan was already way ahead, calling out to the group behind him. He seemed over the moon to have been picked as our leader. Esther and I trailed at the back. Mud sucked our shoes, the tip of Esther's cane.

She leaned in, her voice low, so only I could hear her.

'I've had enough of this. I'm getting the fuck out.'

Esther wasn't at lunch. Karma was also missing.

Faith barely touched her soup. She didn't want to talk about what happened. I tried chatting to her about other stuff, but our conversation quickly petered out, and I found myself watching the other guests. Scream therapy had loosened them up, made them more talkative, whereas Faith and I were silent and rigid in our seats.

The door was behind my chair, and I heard raised voices coming from the entrance hall. I strained to listen over the blare of people's chatter and laughter. It was Esther and Karma. Esther insisting on calling a taxi. Karma saying that wasn't possible. Esther shouting about being kept here against her will.

A door slammed, and their voices disappeared.

I didn't see Esther for the rest of the day, and I thought she must have got her way and gone home. Noah took the rest of us on a walk around Murkwater, which wasn't as nice as usual. The sky was overcast and dull, and a blustery wind threw the stench of rotting fish in our faces, making our eyes water.

On the way back, we passed the goats and chickens, staff mucking out the coop. They were intent on their work, not registering us. We passed the wooden shack, its door ajar. Another gust hit me, carrying the iron-rich smell of a butcher's, of meat dangling on hooks.

That night, I waited up for Faith, hoping she'd talk to me properly when we were alone. There was no sign of her.

Toxic People helped me pass the time. On a blank page, J.B. had drawn a map of the retreat – Blundale Hall, the woods and crop fields and animal enclosures, complete with tiny goats and chickens. Kidney-shaped Murkwater, with little ripple lines in the body of the lake. In one corner of the woods, they'd drawn trees with ears, marked JUDAS TREES. An arrow pointed west towards GATE, then onto a road, leading to THE ELIXIR. Along the arrow, J.B. had written PATH TO DAMNATION.

As I studied the map, the house stirred. Floorboards creaked. Doors slammed shut. Feet scurried across the landing, up and down the stairs.

What was going on? Where was Faith? I got up to investigate.

When I opened the bedroom door, Faith was on the other side, about to come in.

'What are you doing?' she said.

'Coming to find you. Where've you been?'

'Working.'

She pushed past me and slumped onto her bed. She hadn't washed her hair for several days, and it fell around her face, lank and greasy. Her lips were chapped, nails bitten.

I perched on the edge of her bed and tapped her arm gently. 'Are you okay?'

She shook my hand away as if a bug had landed on her. Scratched the patch of skin I'd touched.

'Leave me the fuck alone,' she said.

It hurt, how much I repelled her. I flounced to my own bed, tired of her mood swings, of not knowing where I stood with her from one moment to the next.

'So much for us being friends,' I blurted out.

She burst out laughing, her mouth twisting into a horrible smile.

'Some friend you've been.'

My face burned. Rage and guilt fought inside me until I didn't know what to feel. My throat tightened – the closest sensation to a flare-up since I'd arrived here. I began to mumble an apology just to diffuse the situation, to stop her smiling at me like that, but Faith said she wanted to go to bed and turned out the lights.

For the rest of the night, I lay awake, replaying her words in my head. The contempt in them.

I got up before Faith, not wanting to be around when she woke up, and went down to the dining hall. I was surprised to find Esther at the table. She looked different – she wasn't wearing her glasses. Her face looked bare without the chunky pink frames. When I waved from the door, she didn't wave back, but maybe she hadn't seen properly.

I sat next to her. 'Are you okay?'

Normally, when I asked Esther how she was, she'd shrug, say something stoical. Not bad. Can't complain.

That morning, she turned to me with a smile. 'Great, thanks.'

Her smile didn't reach her eyes, which were bloodshot, smaller without her glasses on.

Faith came in and took a seat at the other end of the table. I avoided looking in her direction.

Esther didn't complain when they gave us one boiled egg instead of two and no toast, or when she broke into her egg and the yolk was dry. She gazed at it, not eating.

I lowered my voice. 'Where were you yesterday? After scream therapy?'

'Oh, that. I wasn't feeling well. Bit mixed up, you know. Karma took me to see Charles.'

'I thought you'd gone home.'

Karma sat in the chair opposite, and Esther's eyes darted to her for a second, before focusing on me again. She laughed.

'Course not. I'm staying. It's the only way I'll get rid of the arthritis.'

'Where are your glasses? Your cane?' It wasn't hooked over the back of her chair like usual.

'Charles said I won't need them anymore. Not if I put the work in.'

The next chapter in *Toxic People* was about relationships.

Toxic relationships unleash havoc on the body, spawning cancerous cells, inflammation, and immune function impairment. It is vitally important for health to reduce contact with toxic influences or cut ties altogether.

J.B. had underlined these sentences and scribbled: mum and dad.

I thought about toxic influences in my own life. My parents. Mark. Nate.

Faith.

When we were kids, she'd been controlling, bossy, possessive. If she hadn't been like that, I might not have ended up with Nate, clinging to him in the same way. Had she never been in my life, I might have been a better person. Stronger, healthier.

We were back on speaking terms again, pretending nothing had happened, which seemed the only way to get through living in close quarters. But I started to look at her differently.

Once you start seeing the world through a particular lens, it's hard to see any other way.

Visitations

FOLLOWING SEVERAL CONVERSATIONS WITH Lucy, I am getting a sense of the world Julie stepped into when she joined the retreat. The world that engulfed her.

Lucy says her chronic cough is getting worse, along with the after-effects: pain, fatigue, anxiety and depression. 'Have you been to see the doctor?' I've asked; a reasonable question given the circumstances. Surely, after her experiences at the retreat, she must see that the only sensible course of action is to seek medical attention from a qualified and licensed practitioner. She won't give me a straight answer, either changing the subject or saying something cryptic. 'I already know why it's getting worse.'

I worry Hartman's rubbish hasn't washed out of her system.

On several occasions, she hasn't joined our Skype call as planned, cancelled last minute, or cut the meeting short.

'I saw Noah today,' she told me during our call a few days ago. 'I'm sure it was him. Driving the minivan.'

I was sceptical. One sees any number of fat bearded men in white vans on any given day.

'They've been calling me, too,' she went on, breathlessly. 'Day and night. When I answer, it's silent for a few seconds and then the line goes dead. Mark's livid. I don't know how they got his landline number, how they know I'm living here.'

Again, I made a rational counterargument: these were merely run-of-the-mill spam calls. I'd had several such nuisance calls myself, recently; a sign of the times, a symptom of austerity. Despite offering these reasonable suggestions, Lucy was too upset to speak further and terminated our call. It's a frustrating setback, but I must be patient.

Reader, I'll be frank. I've been remiss in my investigations. For too long, I neglected a key witness: someone close to Julie, who might shed more light on her final days. Even without my current project, I should have reached out to this person years ago. It shouldn't have taken finding Julie's letters at Mum and Dad's house, and re-examining the circumstances leading up to Julie's death, to make contact with her. Truthfully, I was reluctant and afraid to do so sooner.

It wasn't difficult to find her. It took about five seconds, in fact, to track her down on Facebook. She still lives in Salford.

I tried not to hope for much. Claire was within her rights to ignore my Facebook 'Friend' request, after how my family and I had treated her. She had been best friends with Julie since infant school. We should have kept her close. And yet, by common, unspoken agreement, my siblings and I distanced ourselves from Claire and her mother after Julie's death. Mum was furious with them: furious with Claire for allowing Julie to stay at her flat when Julie should have come straight home, or so my mother thought; furious with Jackie for not telling Mum sooner that Julie was at Claire's. To be sure, the rest of the family did not believe that Mum's anger was well-directed, but we were grieving, and too exhausted to disagree. We took Mum's side.

So, I was surprised when Claire accepted my Facebook request and invited me over for a brew. It shouldn't have been surprising, really; Claire always was a pleasant girl.

She was even happy for me to bring John Snow when I explained I didn't like leaving him alone at home for too long. She proceeded to send me a barrage of photos of her own three dogs, entirely unsolicited.

On my way to Claire's house in Walkden, while John Snow snuffled in the back seat, I couldn't help but notice a white minivan in my rear-view mirror. Lucy had only mentioned seeing Noah a few days ago, or so she believed, and here I was, paying close attention to the van following me, when at any other time I wouldn't have even registered it. It's fascinating, how the human brain works – our susceptibility to the power of suggestion, how easily we can be persuaded of some warped reality. Similarly, our vulnerability to cognitive dissonance – the cult survivors' support group mentioned this term – how we tend to overlook uncomfortable

truths. I am beginning to understand why Olivia wanted to read psychology at university, although I hadn't
been in favour of her decision previously. I used to think
psychology was a soft subject, a pseudoscience.

Claire welcomed me into her home with a hug, a reception I surely did not deserve, while our dogs barked
at each other companionably and scurried around our
feet. She's much larger now; whatever physical attrac-
tiveness she might have had at one time has long since
faded. Yet she remains as friendly and outgoing as ever;
a warm, uncomplicated, wholesome sort of person. I
used to think she was a good influence on Julie in this
regard, given Julie's tendency towards introspection
and melancholy.

Photos of her three sons at various ages lined the
walls and mantelpiece of her small, cosy living room
where, on the coffee table, she placed two large mugs of
tea and a plate of chocolate biscuits. Perched on the edge
of the sofa, I sipped my tea, unusually taciturn, unable
to say what needed to be said. She asked after Jen and
Olivia, my siblings, my parents. I explained Mum had
recently passed away. If she felt any lingering resentment
towards Mum, she didn't show it.

She brought out a photo album and flipped through
the silky plastic sleeves until she found what she was
looking for: a photo of Julie in her twenties, with black,
backcombed hair, black eyeshadow, a leather miniskirt,
and a fishnet top – clothes she was forbidden from
wearing under my parents' roof – sticking out her

pierced tongue at the camera. It's a version of Julie you won't find in any of my family's photo albums.

Claire pulled the photo out of its sleeve and handed it to me. 'I thought you might like to have it,' she said, her eyes welling up.

John Snow pattered over and rested his head on my knee, apparently intuiting the additional strength his master needed for this difficult conversation. It was at that moment when I bit the bullet and apologised to Claire for how my family and I had cut her off. She was incredibly forgiving.

'It was such a terrible shock when she died. You must have been devastated,' she said, squeezing my hand. My shame deepened: Claire must have been devastated, too.

I told her about discovering Julie's letters, my research into the retreat, and my book-in-progress. Claire looked alarmed.

'I hope you're being careful,' she said. I pressed her to explain what she meant.

She told me that Julie had called her, out of the blue, in December 1993. 'She hadn't written to me for almost a year, and then suddenly she was calling me from a pub in Cumbria.' Julie arrived outside her door a couple of hours later, asking Claire to pay the taxi driver waiting outside.

'She was in such a state, Richard, you should have seen her. But she made me promise not to tell anyone she'd come back.'

Julie was emaciated. She complained of terrible stomach cramps. Claire tried to get her to eat more. 'It was like she was afraid of food – just regular food, like bread or fruit, because it wasn't from this place she'd been living in. She didn't even want tap water. She asked me to buy her bottled spring water from Cumbria. That was all she drank.'

Julie wouldn't talk about the retreat, or Charles. But she kept talking about someone called Michael.

'She said he was angry with her. She wouldn't tell me what she was supposed to have done wrong. She seemed afraid of him. I kept telling her to go to the police, but she said they wouldn't be able to do anything to stop him.'

Claire tried to get Julie to speak to Mum and Dad; Julie resisted, insisting they wouldn't want anything to do with her anymore. 'My mum lost patience, in the end, and went round to tell your mum that Julie was back. Julie went ballistic when she found out, but it did prompt her to make contact.'

On the few occasions Claire managed to persuade Julie to leave the house, Julie got paranoid. She thought she recognised people from the retreat following her.

'One day, two blokes knocked on my door. They said they were friends of Julie's. Seemed nice enough. Polite. I went into Julie's room and asked her if I should let them in, but she said not to. They were from the retreat. I went back to give them a piece of my mind, but they'd already left.'

Then there were the phone calls. 'They'd wake me up in the middle of the night. As soon as I answered, the line went dead.'

Claire came home from work one day and heard Julie shouting down the phone: 'I don't care what I did to him. You tell him, I'm going to the police. I'll tell them everything!'

It was the only time Julie seemed to genuinely consider going to the police. 'She was so riled up by that phone call. I was relieved. She sounded like herself again. The real Julie. The fighter.'

But Julie never went to the police. A few days later, Claire came home and found Julie dead.

She began sobbing as she told me this; twenty years had gone by, and it was still just as painful.

'I told the police about the people who'd been harassing her. How I suspected she'd been abused at the retreat. But I didn't have any proof. And there was no evidence that anyone had broken in or anything. Everyone thought she'd killed herself. Even my mum didn't believe when I said Julie had been murdered.'

The word shocked me: a possibility I'd never considered before. It seemed far-fetched. Hartman manipulated and conned people, certainly. But cold-blooded murder?

I kept quiet, wanting to let her speak.

'I tried to talk to your mum about it, but she wouldn't listen. She said if anyone had murdered Julie, it was me. That it was my fault Julie died, because I didn't tell her she was back, so Julie didn't get the help she needed. She was right, I should have told her. Maybe Julie would still be alive if I had.'

At the end of our reunion, I promised to keep in touch with Claire and let her know when I finished my book. She said she couldn't wait to read it; Julie's story needed to be heard.

'Just mind how you go investigating those people,' she said. 'I'm worried what they'll do if they find out.'

Transcript Excerpt #4

ME: Can we talk about Michael?

> *[Lucy doesn't answer. She looks away
> from the screen, a pained look on her
> face. She starts to cough and mutes her
> mic.]*

ME: Lucy? Was there someone called Michael at the
retreat? You've said his name a few times, and Julie
spoke of someone called Michael when she came
back. She said she'd made him angry. She was afraid
of him.

[Lucy turns her mic back on, clears her throat.]

LUCY: We all were.

ME: Why?

LUCY: He... *[PAUSE]* I can't. I can't do this. Sorry.

ME: Why not?

LUCY: I just can't. We're not supposed to talk about
him. I shouldn't even have said his name. It's sacred.

ME: You said you weren't supposed talk about the retreat at all, but you wanted to get the truth out.
You wanted to help me understand what Julie went
through.

LUCY: I do want to help. It's just ... I'm scared.

ME: Well, I won't push it. But I'd be extremely grateful because, frankly, I don't understand. Julie said
Michael was angry at her, so I thought he might have
had something to do with her death. But he's not
real, is he?

LUCY: He _is_ real. I've seen him.

Lucy

CHARLES DOESN'T WRITE ABOUT Michael in *Toxic People*, although he does in *Spirit of the Mountain* and *Blessed*. I read both in the library that summer, as well as re-reading *Toxic People*, which lived on my bedside table – I thought if I kept the book close to me and learned it by heart, I might heal faster. My cough hadn't returned, but in my consultations, Charles recommended staying longer.

'In some areas the disease is in remission. But in others...' He sighed, pushed his glasses up his nose. 'Let's just say you still have a long way to go.'

I was stumped – I'd been doing all the activities, plus extra reading. 'What else can I do?'

'I think you're ready to take the next step. To join the Purges.'

He didn't explain what the Purges were, just that they'd help me ascend into a purer state. Eliminate toxic thinking.

'Crucial for any Healer-in-training,' he added, stroking my face.

Each night before going to sleep – I'd stopped waiting up for Faith – I'd return to *Toxic People*. J.B. had written Michael's name on dozens of pages, always inside a wreath of stars.

I found notes I hadn't spotted on my first reading, including a faint scribble on a page corner that had been folded down. `read closely`. Another note was squeezed into the centre margin, which I only discovered by flattening the pages. The blue ink was barely visible, fading in and out.

`true healing empowers you. charles hartman overcame pain. uncovered perfection, truth, health, enlightenment. became omnipotent, divine, immortal. eradicated sickness.`

It reminded me of the note in the scream therapy section. The same frenzied tone.

I'd liked the annotations at first. J.B. was my pen pal from the past, my mentor, guiding me towards important passages. But they began to bother me, especially when I found the markings inside the dust jacket. The jacket was falling apart, so I pulled it off to leave on my bedside table, until I noticed scratches on the blank side, concentrated in the area behind Charles's photo. Some so deep they'd pierced the paper. I had to hold the blank side under a bright light to see the scratches were words.

`liar`
`rapist`
`murderer`

I flung it away from me, watched it slide under Faith's bedside table. Those words brought to mind things I didn't want to think about, making me see them in a new, harsh, unforgiving light. The guests with life-threatening illnesses whom Charles had told to cancel surgeries and stop taking medications, promising he'd cure them at the retreat. The guests who took a turn for the worse, gone the next day. 'They didn't do the treatment properly,' Karma would say if anyone asked why. 'Didn't change their toxic ways.' How Charles had been making me undress for my consultations, telling me to lie back and open my legs for him to examine me. Sliding his hand between my thighs. There was a tumour in there, he said, a stubborn tumour that would keep growing if I left. He was saving me.

I had to keep believing that, because the alternative was too devastating.

The dust jacket had disappeared from view, and part of me wanted to leave it there. Out of sight, out of mind. But I also didn't want Faith to find it, see those ugly, blasphemous words – what if she thought I wrote them? What would she do? I crouched down and reached into the narrow gap between the bottom of the bedside table and the floor, felt the scuffed edge of the paper.

'What are you doing?'

I hadn't heard her come in. She slammed the door behind her and rushed over, squeezing herself between me and the table. A barrier.

I stood up, holding up the dust jacket. 'It fell off my book. I was just getting it back.'

'Right. Whatever.'

What residues of trust there'd been between us had disintegrated. She was constantly on my back, pointing out my flaws. 'That's toxic thinking,' she'd say, if I made a comment that wasn't to her liking – something trivial, like the weather being too hot, or feeling hungry or tired, or complaining about my skin itching after we'd gone swimming in Murkwater. She'd shame me for admitting these things, despite the sunburn on her nose, the hollows in her cheeks and bags under her eyes, the rashes on her arms and legs. As the weeks rolled on, I began to bite back.

'Look at the state of your arm,' I said, pointing at the angry red welts where she'd scratched too hard. 'You're not supposed to touch the rashes. That's your body shedding toxins. You're supposed to let them heal.'

Whenever she chastised me over something small, I reminded myself that she was the one who'd fucked up. She'd left the retreat despite Charles warning her not to. She'd made her illness worse. Ever since she'd lost it in scream therapy, the rest of the group had avoided her, worried whatever excess of toxicity she'd revealed then might be contagious. Her mistakes were often the subject of the Purges.

Esther and I joined the Purges that summer, when we'd already been at the retreat a few months. They began at midnight and lasted for hours, sometimes until sunrise, and we'd be expected to go to breakfast without any sleep. I realised that was why Faith came to bed late some nights, or not at all, and would only tell me she'd been volunteering. The Purges were a secret, honoured ritual, an intense therapy only offered to long-term guests deemed sufficiently committed to their health. On a Purge night, Karma would come round to each of us at dinner and whisper in our ears to wait behind in the entrance hall afterwards, not go up to bed.

Whenever Charles led the Purges, Faith took more care with her appearance, combing her fingers through her hair until it was shiny and smooth, checking her reflection in the entrance hall mirror before we filed into the drawing room.

Karma noticed her doing this and nudged her along, chiding like a teacher. 'Stop messing with that hair.'

Karma led the purges if Charles wasn't around. He'd disappear for days, and she'd tell us he was 'away on business.' We'd mope until he returned, when we'd burst into frenzy, like dogs when their owner gets home.

In the drawing room, we moved aside the tables and chairs, which we used in art therapy sessions during the day, and sat on the floor in a circle. You burnt your back if you sat too close to the fireplace or shivered if you sat near the windows – even in summer, there was a cold draught. Charles sat in the comfortable area in between on a silk cushion. Smoke poured from incense sticks, filling the room with the scent of sandalwood. Candles flickered, burning out as the hours dragged on. Shadows danced across the walls, across our clumsy paintings of Lyfell Pike, the results of our art therapy sessions.

They looked even worse next to the portraits of saints, which were expertly done, beautiful and disturbing at the same time. A man who'd been tied to a tree and shot with arrows. A woman with severed breasts. A woman carrying a pair of eyes on a plate.

Charles would pick someone to Purge first. This person would confess something they were ashamed of doing. Cheating on their partner. Working in a job they hated because it was what their parents wanted. Drinking too much, binge-eating, not looking after themselves. The rest of the group had to identify why their behaviour was toxic. You'd shout things out. 'Slut!' 'People pleaser!' 'Weak!' 'Lazy!' Then the group would decide if confession was enough to purge their toxicity, or if some form of penance was required.

Penance might be taking a vow of silence or going without food or sleep for a week. Sleeping in the goat pen, with other animals who wallowed in their own filth.

When Dan confessed he'd only stayed married out of fear of being alone, until his wife asked for a divorce, Clover suggested locking him inside the sensory deprivation tank. He begged us not to – he was claustrophobic. But Charles agreed with Clover, explaining penance must be *contrapasso*. 'To purge neurological toxicity, one must undergo a detox that resembles or contrasts the toxic behaviour. Dan clung to a toxic marriage because he was afraid of solitude. So, he should face being truly alone.'

The trick was to confess something bad enough that it warranted purging. Because if it was only a mild indiscretion, or if Charles suspected you of sanitising – justifying your behaviour, making yourself look better than you actually were – this was automatic grounds for penance.

I had plenty to confess, plenty to feel bad about. Staying with Nate long after our relationship had run its course, because it seemed easier than breaking up. Being a workaholic because I wanted to feel important and needed, even though it made no difference – my patients still got ill and died. Keeping my parents at a distance, because I was afraid of being honest with them about how angry I was – angry they'd always loved my brother more than me. When I purged, the group shouted at me. 'Coward!' 'Narcissist!' 'Liar!'

It took me weeks to work up to what I felt guiltiest about.

'I let my boyfriend take over my life and abandoned my best friend, even when she got ill.'

I looked at Faith when I finished, resigned to whatever terrible penance she'd suggest. But Charles spoke up before anyone else. His voice was gentle, a salve.

'You're being too hard on yourself, Lucy. Friends can be bad for us. Whoever this friend was, she was ill for good reason. She was toxic.'

The group murmured in agreement, and Charles picked someone else to go next.

That was it? The worst thing I ever did, and Charles brushed it aside, like it was nothing.

I couldn't look at Faith.

When it was her turn to purge, Charles interrupted her partway.

He made his voice shrill. Mimicking her. *'Wah, my daddy left me. I had cancer. Mummy's ill.'*

She hadn't said anything about these things during her purge, so I wondered if he was referring to stuff she'd told him during her consultations. In confidence.

He switched to his regular voice. 'There's self-pity in everything you say. Blaming everyone else, taking no responsibility for your own toxic behaviour. You say your mother made you have chemo when you were eighteen. Legally, an adult. Take some responsibility. You made that choice, just like you did when you chose to leave here against my recommendation. Your illness is your fault.'

As penance, Charles told us to shun her for a week. We weren't supposed to even look at her. We had to act like she didn't exist – her punishment for not taking responsibility for her own existence.

At night, I heard her crying, quietly. Part of me wanted go over to her bed, hold her hand, talk to her. But I was afraid Charles would find out. Maybe she'd tell him.

I rolled over, pretending to be asleep.

One night, we were called to the drawing room for what I thought was another Purge.

Charles told us to sit in a circle as usual, except this time he remained standing. Faith pushed her way to the front to claim the spot directly in front of him. I traipsed in last, taking the spot behind him. I'd been feeling queasy since dinner – the food tasted off – and I hoped the Purge wouldn't go on for too long.

His voice was quiet, forbidding, as he surveyed the guests sat in front of him. 'Do you think I'm a fool? I know some of you are being dishonest with me.'

The colour drained from Faith's cheeks, although Charles didn't seem to be speaking to her directly.

'I welcome you here, treat you as family. And this is how you repay me. Keeping secrets. Running home, then crawling back. Saying you want to get healthy, then clinging to toxicity. Feeding on it. Fucking maggots.'

Where was the kindly, smiling Charles who welcomed us into his consultation room, who led us up the mountain? We glanced around at each other, suspicious of everyone in the circle, whoever might be responsible for bringing out this other, terrible Charles. At the same time, I felt personally responsible, sick to my stomach with guilt, even though I didn't know what I'd done wrong.

'You see this?' He pointed to the scar on his lip. 'Years ago, I treated a young woman with all my power and love. With Michael's love. And after everything I did for her, she did this to me. Stabbed me with a pen. Left her toxic mark. A wound like that never heals on a pure being. But it was much worse for her, after she left. I decided then I'd never let that happen again. Never let another one of my charges succumb to their own toxicity.'

He walked around the circle, staring down at each of us, rooting out the toxic ones.

'Because of the liars among you, everyone's recovery is compromised. You've all been contaminated. I must summon Michael to cleanse you.'

There was pandemonium. Almost everyone in the circle broke down and wept. Dan begged. 'Please, no, not Michael. Please, Charles. Please.' Faith looked like she was about to faint.

Esther and I looked at each other, confused. During mountain bathing, Charles would ask for Michael's blessing before he cleansed us. I'd taken Michael to be a benevolent spirit. So why was everyone terrified?

Charles shouted at us to shut up. Everyone fell silent. He drew a candle and a lighter out of his pockets and lit the candle as he spoke.

'I call upon the great spirit Michael to bring you back to the path of health. To show what will happen if you stray.'

Yellow-green halos floated across my eyes, wherever I looked. I blinked, but they wouldn't disappear, circling around the candle as I watched the flame begin to flicker in all directions.

In my peripheral vision – a ribbon of shimmering light, from which a shape was emerging, bending the air, extending long fingers.

I tried to stand, run, but my knees buckled at the sudden, terrible pain in my chest, squeezing like a vice.

My lungs had collapsed. I was coughing, wheezing, unable to breathe. My hands flitted to my neck, where I felt the cancerous mass through my skin, hard as a pebble, lodged in my throat. I looked around wildly for someone, anyone, to help me.

My eyes met Faith's.

Her eyes pleaded to me from two tunnels deep inside her head, now all but a skull. She opened her lipless mouth, tried to speak. No voice came out. Her emaciated body was covered in lumps, with the largest, darkest swellings protruding from her neck. Their stench hit me from across the room – the sickly-sweet smell of rot.

They were all around the room, these living corpses. Grey-skinned and wailing. Clover dragged herself across the floor with her hands, her legs trailing behind her. Esther writhed in pain, clutching her swollen joints, which had contorted her limbs into strange angles. Dan babbled psychotically about things only he could see. Flea-ridden rats scurrying up his legs. A monk watching from outside the window, whose long, long face was hidden beneath a cowl.

The cleansing went on all night, until Charles and Michael were satisfied that we understood what was at stake. What would happen if we succumbed to our own toxicity.

None of us wanted Charles to have to summon Michael ever again.

Transcript Excerpt #5

ME: It wasn't real. Lucy? They must have drugged the
   food.
LUCY: I've seen him again since I left. The rings of
   light. This – this figure, reaching at me.

[She begins to cry.]

ME: It's probably PTSD. Something like that. My
   daughter, Olivia, she gets these migraines, sees flash-
   ing lights—
LUCY: Yeah, I know what migraines are. I've never had
   migraines.
ME: What I'm saying is, whatever you think you've
   seen, it's not real.
LUCY: How do you know?
ME: I know Charles was manipulating you. He made
   Michael up. It's a bogeyman, a fairy tale to keep you
   in line.
LUCY: How come my illness is getting worse, then?
   I went back to the doctor, like you suggested, and

they just offered me antidepressants. Even though I can feel it in my throat. The lump. *[She coughs again, sips some water.]* I'm sick of people telling me it's all in my head. Charles conned me, I get that. But my cough disappeared at the retreat. That was real.

ME: Or was it just a placebo effect? Or drugs, like I said. Come on, Lucy. Don't let them fool you. That's exactly what they did to Julie, scaring her, making her think they were coming after her.

LUCY: They <u>have</u> been following me. Calling the house.

ME: Isn't it very possible you imagined it?

LUCY: Look, I need to go, Richard.

ME: Stay a little longer, please. How about we discuss something else? Your escape?

LUCY: I'm too tired for this right now, okay? Let's pick this up another time.

[She ends the call abruptly, leaving me staring at my own face in the screen.]

Lucy

At reception, Karma told me there was an issue with extending my stay. I'd just come out of another consultation with Charles, who'd recommended at least another month or two – this was a critical time in my healing.

'Declined,' she said, holding up my debit card.

'There must be an issue with it. I'll call the bank if you give me my phone back.'

'I think you've run out of money, pet.' She shook her head at my carelessness.

She asked if I had another way to pay. I had some money in a savings account, leftover inheritance from my parents. The rest was tied up in the London flat I'd bought with Nate, where he still lived – we'd never finalised a schedule for him to buy me out of my share. I gave her my bank details to access my savings.

'There's not much left. I might have to come back when I've got more money.' As I said this, my mouth went dry. I couldn't leave. It would be catastrophic for my health.

'Where will you get money from?'

'I'll go back to work.'

'You resigned.'

She showed me a photocopy of a resignation letter dated weeks earlier, addressed to the hospice.

I stared at it, bewildered. 'I didn't write that.'

'What, the letter signed itself?' She pointed at the signature, unmistakably mine.

I had no memory of signing it, but I was struggling to remember much at all from the last few weeks. The days blurred together, an endless rotation of mountain bathing, yoga, art therapy, scream therapy, private consultations, Purges. Mealtimes with meagre portions, except when newcomers came. On the day they arrived, it was like a holiday, with the Welcome Feast – I'd stuff my face at the buffet, gorge myself until I felt sick. It was the only time we all had plenty of food. And there were no Purges afterwards.

Karma asked if there was anyone I could borrow money from – friends, family. 'Or you could offer a pledge.'

'What's that?' A spark of recognition in my foggy brain. Noah had asked if I was Faith's pledge when he picked us up from Penrith.

'Someone else who's likely to commit to treatment long term. We'll give you a discount for as long as they stay.'

So, that's what I'd been. Faith's cut-rate ticket back to the retreat. Was that the only reason she'd reconnected with me?

I pushed the question out of my head, trying to focus on the pressing matter at hand. 'What about volunteering? Can I stay for free if I volunteer?'

'If you're willing to work hard, yes. That can be arranged.'

I was assigned more chores than Faith: cleaning, cooking, harvesting. Mucking out the goat pen and the chicken coop. Gutting fish. On top of this, I was still expected to attend as many activities as possible, plus Purges and private consultations.

Later, I found out all the staff were volunteers. No one got paid for their work, not even Karma, Charles's long-time apprentice. Noah had a few perks – the van, a stipend to keep it running, and the freedom to drive away from Blundale, apparently without harming his health. He and Charles often left for days.

The rest of us would be risking our lives if we left.

I was too exhausted to dwell on the inconsistencies and hypocrisies. I explained them away: Charles, our Master Healer, had ascended to the purest state of being, making him immune to the toxic environment beyond the retreat's boundaries. Noah and Karma, who'd been here longest, were further along in their healing than the rest of us, giving them some level of immunity, although Karma stayed to run the retreat in Charles's absence as his trusted assistant.

Similarly, I tried not to linger over my suspicion that J.B. was the one who'd attacked Charles. Who'd given him that scar. J.B.'s book stayed on my bedside table as before, in its mouldering dust jacket, unassuming from the outside, hiding its corruption within. I used to think reading it might heal me faster – now I worried it was slowing my recovery. Why not get rid of it? Putting it back in the library risked its profane notes harming someone else. Handing it over to Karma would draw attention and raise questions about why I'd kept it for so long. Binning it risked me getting caught, raising more questions.

So, I kept it close. There were other reasons I wouldn't admit to myself at the time. When I had a couple of minutes to myself, I pulled off the dust jacket to gaze at those marks puncturing the back of Charles's photo and savour a small thrill – no one else, including Charles, knew they were there. I had a revolted fascination with them, like a horrible wound I couldn't look away from – a patient pulling off their socks to reveal gangrenous, blackened toes.

The orchard turned golden-yellow, and apples fell, skins splitting as they hit the ground, insides oozing, festering at our feet. Mushrooms sprang up everywhere. Noah pointed them out on our group foraging walks – oyster, morel, hen of the woods, liberty cap. Some resembled body parts. The ones that looked like breasts, or eyes, with dark circles at the centre of their domes, were parasol mushrooms. The red hands reaching through the grass, devil's fingers. Deeper into the woods, we found a patch of dead elder trees, their bark covered in ears.

'Judas ears,' said Noah, touching one of the fleshy growths, their delicate, cupped shape like cartilage. 'Named after Judas from the Bible, who hanged himself after betraying Christ.'

J.B.'s map of the retreat immediately came to mind. The arrow pointing west from the JUDAS TREES, towards GATE and THE ELIXIR beyond.

PATH TO DAMNATION

I carried on walking past the dead trees, in the direction I guessed was west from the direction of the sun, until Noah called me back.

After filling our baskets with mushrooms, apples, and blackberries, we headed back to the house, trying to resist helping ourselves. Snacking outside of meals was forbidden. All our findings had to be delivered to the kitchen. Still, a few blackberries found their way into our pockets.

In our bathroom, the mushrooms around the window multiplied. The week I fasted – penance for having eaten junk food in my past – when I was doubling over with hunger pains, I pulled one of those mushrooms off the wall and crammed it into my mouth. It was cold, moist, chewy. Like eating mouldy meat. I couldn't swallow and spat it into the toilet.

One night, we were called into the drawing room. I found an empty spot on the floor and waited for the Purge to begin.

It wasn't any ordinary Purge.

Karma flung something into the middle of our circle, where it landed on the rug with a thud. Dozens of eyes stared at the object, fearing and coveting it all at once.

A phone.

The screen was dead and had a crack along the bottom, possibly from the impact of the fall.

Karma prowled around us as she spoke.

'This was discovered in the cleaning supplies cupboard. No battery or SIM card. The culprit's hidden those elsewhere. Who does this belong to?'

Her question hung in the air like a noxious gas. I held my breath.

I didn't dare look at anyone in particular. It could be perceived as an accusation – or an admission of guilt.

Karma's glare swept over the group. 'Until the culprit's found, no one leaves this room. They've jeopardised your recovery. The whole time this phone hasn't been sealed away, it's been emitting radiation. Harming everyone. All your work and time and money and energy towards healing have been wasted because of this selfish person.'

The circle erupted with angry murmurs, sighs of agitation and despair. Faith drew her knees up to her forehead and hugged herself into a tight ball. Dan buried his face in his hands. Esther punched the floor. 'I'll fucking kill them,' she spat.

Dan lifted his face and glared around the circle. 'Whoever did this, you might as well come forward before things get ugly.'

Of course, no one came forward.

Karma turned around slowly, surveying each of us. Her gaze fixed on Faith longer than anyone else.

Faith stirred at my side, her hand quivering as she pointed in my direction.

'Lucy was the last person in the cleaning supplies cupboard. I saw her.'

I felt like I'd been sliced at the belly, guts sliding to the floor. Why was she saying this? It wasn't true. Her hand dropped to her lap, where she focused her attention instead of looking me in the eye.

Everyone went quiet. I could hear my frantic pulse in my temples, beating my skull.

Karma stepped closer. 'Lucy? Is it yours?'

'No!' My shout echoed through the room.

Esther piped up in my defence. 'It can't be Lucy's.' But she was narrowing her eyes at me, along with everyone else.

'It's not mine,' I said. I turned to Faith. 'You saw me hand in my phone when we arrived.'

'Then you brought a spare. Hid it under your clothes.'

She came out with this so quickly, it seemed she'd been planning it. Planning to throw me under the bus.

That probably wasn't the case. I realise that now. But at the time, the idea seeded itself in my mind and took root. She'd hated me ever since I'd abandoned our friendship when we were teenagers. She'd only tracked me down because she wanted to exploit me. Now, she wanted to humiliate me. To ruin my chances of recovery by getting me thrown out of the retreat.

I kept my voice steady as best as I could. 'I didn't even know about the phone rule until I got here, after you invited me. You never told me. Why would I bring a secret phone if I didn't know they weren't allowed?'

Her face flushed. Her mouth opened, then closed again, like a fish, as she struggled to come up with a counterargument. She had nothing. I'd nailed her to the cross.

My sad little victory in that desperate place.

If only I'd left it there.

'On the day we got here, when I came out the bathroom, you were messing about with something behind your bedside table. You said it was nothing. But when I dropped something under the table, you got all cagey about me feeling under it. After that, you must have needed a different hiding place.'

I left the implication hanging. Understanding dawned on people's faces.

Faith shook her head. 'That's bullshit. She's lying.'

But everyone was glaring at her, and I couldn't stop.

'When you left the retreat, you tried to get your mum to come here.' I turned to address the room. 'Her mum's got cancer. She's having chemo.'

People flinched at the offensive word. Shouted, 'Poison!'

I carried on. 'Your mum refused. And she tried to talk you into not going back, didn't she? She rang you on the train, when we were on our way here. But you weren't prepared to cut contact with her.'

'Shut up!' Faith screamed. 'You don't know what you're talking about!'

'Enough.' Karma cut us short. She turned to Faith.

'I've had concerns about you for a long time. Your lack of commitment. Toddling off home to your mother. Charles was so good to you, and you didn't deserve it.'

Her mouth wrinkled as though she'd bitten into sour fruit. She walked up to the phone and kicked it. It slid across the floor and hit Faith's shin.

'Admit it.'

Faith crumpled.

When she cried, she looked so tired, so thin and weak. My sense of victory deflated. I'd gone too far.

Part of me wanted to rush to her side and apologise, tell Karma to back off. But I was still reeling from her trying to scapegoat me, and I wanted to fit in with the group, not be cast out.

So, I joined in with the rest as we shouted at Faith to admit what she'd done. She wouldn't, only crying and shaking her head, which spurred us on. We spat on her. Kicked her. Hurled insults like stones.

All that pales in comparison to what we did next.

Karma handed out rope, a sack. Dan and Clover grabbed Faith's arms and tied them behind her back. Esther threw the sack over her head. Karma led us into the entrance hall, and we shunted Faith through the door, out into the cold night.

We came to a stop at the back of the house, near the bins and the septic tank – an area we usually avoided because of the smell. For all we talked about cleansing and purging, we didn't like to be reminded of our own filth.

The outdoor security light on the wall cast a harsh, white light over all of us. The air was thick with drizzle. Our vestments grew heavy with moisture, clinging fast to our soaked skin.

Karma sermonised. She'd seen Charles do it enough times, and she relished taking her turn.

'If the patient's wounded limb turns septic, a surgeon must amputate. Cut off the rotten part before it destroys the whole. Faith, your actions endangered everyone at the retreat. You wallowed in your old life, indulged in toxic influences. You will steep in a place as putrid as you until I sense you're ready to change.'

She commanded us to strip Faith. Before we could pull off her vestments, we had to undo the binds on her wrists and pull off the sack over her head. Her terrified eyes found mine, and she tried to say something, but someone threw the sack back over her, muffling her words.

Was that when I snapped back to myself? Or was it when Noah bent down to unscrew the access hatch on the septic tank?

I watched, transfixed, as Noah prised off the lid and retched – we all did, seconds later, when the stench of raw sewage hit us.

Clover bound Faith's wrists together with the rope and handed the other end to Noah, who jerked it like a leash. Faith lurched towards him, trembling, her bare skin covered in goose pimples. The group shouted at her until she stepped down the hole.

Noah closed the hatch over Faith's head. He left it slightly ajar to keep a flow of oxygen into the tank and allow the rope to snake through the gap, so Clover could tie the end to a tree. To prevent Faith suffocating or drowning.

We followed Karma back inside the house. Meditation was the tonic we needed to cleanse ourselves of exposure to those twin toxins, Faith and her phone. In the drawing room, we lay down, held hands and closed our eyes, while Karma told us to visualise Lyfell Pike, its heavenly stream of healing energy trickling through us.

The whole time, I thought of Faith in the tank. The way she'd looked at me before the hood went back on. I imagined leaping up and sprinting to the tank, lifting the hatch and pulling Faith out. Running away together hand-in-hand, through the woods, until we were far from here.

I didn't get up. I lay motionless on my yoga mat, until sunrise turned the walls golden, and Karma said it was time.

She sent a few people to fetch buckets of water while the rest of us filed outside to the back of the house. Dan prised the hatch off the septic tank. He kept stopping, turning away and spluttering into the crook of his arm. Noah untied the rope around the tree and started pulling.

A blackened, sopping creature emerged through the hole.

I will never forget the smell.

Dark slime dripped down Faith's legs as she staggered towards the tree. Noah covered his nose with one hand, using the other to pull the sack off Faith's head. The others appeared carrying buckets, and we took turns flinging the water at her. Pale skin slowly emerged beneath the slurry. Her protruding ribs and hipbones. Her hair, plastered around her gaunt face.

She fell down and vomited, again and again, long after she had nothing left to bring up.

Even after she'd washed herself with lavender soap, the foul smell clung to her.

When she shuffled into the dining hall halfway through breakfast, head down, people couldn't carry on eating. I hadn't been able to eat anyway. I felt too sick.

Karma stood up, addressing the group. 'Faith can't be cleansed until she gets rid of all that vanity.'

Then she turned to me and gave an order that made my blood turn cold. 'It'll help her heal,' she insisted when I hesitated. 'Don't you want her to get better?'

We went into the entrance hall, where Karma ordered Faith to sit. She didn't resist. It was like she'd been lobotomised, the way she slumped into the chair, gazing at nothing, not all there. Everyone else stood around in a circle, holding hands, swaying left, then right. Singing a hymn to Charles and Michael, our saviours.

I stood behind the chair and took the pair of scissors Karma thrust towards me, my hands shaking as I gathered lengths of Faith's glossy hair between the blades.

The next morning, Faith stayed in bed. She wouldn't get up.

Her breath was shallow, her pulse faint. I considered asking for help, but I didn't know if Charles was back yet, and the thought of going to Karma or anyone else from the group terrified me. Illness wasn't possible here, unless you persisted in toxic thinking. What if they decided further penance was necessary?

She twitched feverishly, her shorn head rolling about on the pillow, the curves and indentations of her skull visible beneath her scalp.

I skimmed through *Toxic People*, looking for guidance, but it was useless. My thumb caught the dog-eared page with J.B.'s note beneath the folded corner. `read closely`. I'd thought J.B. meant the printed text – now I wondered if they meant something else. That strange note squeezed into the centre margin. I read it again, then flipped back to the complementary therapies chapter and re-read the similar note there. I read them together. Read backwards. Read the first letter of each word in both notes, ignoring the punctuation.

They spelled out messages.

I threw the book down and ran to the bathroom to be sick, thinking of those guests who'd gotten worse instead of better, who'd left the next day.

Only, they'd never left.

When I went back into the bedroom, Faith's bedcovers had slid onto the floor. She was shivering violently, covered in sweat. One hand flailed down the side of the bed, trying to grasp the duvet. I picked it up for her, but it was wet through. I let it fall back to the floor and grabbed my duvet instead, tried to cover her with it. She shook her head.

'I don't feel good.'

I helped her to the toilet, held her while she threw up into the bowl.

If she got worse, she'd need to go to hospital. No one here would take her. They wouldn't call an ambulance. If Charles couldn't save her, they'd rather let her die and hide the evidence than let anything challenge their beliefs.

I had to make sure she got better.

I tried to remember my nursing training. She was dehydrated. Malnourished. Probably fighting off infection.

I went downstairs, told everyone Faith was absolutely fine, only resting, letting the detox do its work. I convinced Karma to let her stay in bed with fresh sheets. 'She's doing well, sweating out the toxins.' During kitchen duty, I sneaked bread into my pockets, took jugs of soup upstairs. If anyone asked what I was doing, where Faith was, why she wouldn't come out of our room, I'd say, 'She's quarantining until she's purged her toxicity.'

I stayed with her whenever I could, feeding her, bathing her, helping her to the bathroom – this person I'd known my whole life, as dear and familiar to me and as taken for granted as my own body.

I didn't sleep.

One morning, after breakfast, I came back with a cup of water and a piece of toast for Faith. When I opened the door, she was up, making her bed. I shielded my eyes – she'd opened the curtains, saturating the room with sunlight.

She turned around, beaming.

'I'm wonderful,' she said, after I asked how she was feeling. Her head looked smaller without her hair, her cheekbones more prominent, the hollows beneath them deeper. She took my hands in hers. Her fingers were cold, corpselike.

'Thank you for helping me, Lucy.'

'Don't.' Her words shamed me. I'd expected her to scream at me, attack me after what I'd done to her, what I'd allowed to happen. Not this. 'I had to make sure you recovered.'

'I meant for what you did the other day. Making sure I did penance. Putting me on the right path.'

I couldn't believe what she was saying. I tried to tell her what I'd discovered, how we needed to get out of here.

'But Charles saved me.' Her eyes had turned glassy. 'I've only survived because of Charles. He's been up on the mountain, channelling its energy to me. Passing on Michael's blessing.'

Nothing I said made any difference. She was convinced she was in the safest, healthiest place on earth, that leaving meant death.

I had to get out before it was too late.

I studied J.B.'s map. Hatched a plan.

I considered telling Esther. But I couldn't trust her. If Faith's penance had snapped me back to reality, it had only pushed Esther deeper under the surface. She now quoted entire paragraphs from *Toxic People*.

I left J.B.'s book on Faith's bedside table and encouraged her to read closely, let its contents heal her.

The next time Noah took us foraging, we layered up in coats, gloves and scarves. In the woods, we hunted for signs of life. The trees had turned skeletal, and our boots sank into the dark pulp of decomposing leaves, a shroud over all the dead things buried beneath.

When we reached the trees covered in ears, I slowed my pace, gradually increasing my distance from the group. Dan was pressing ahead as usual, rambling on about Charles, and the others were distracted by him talking, oblivious to me edging away.

The rest of the group was a way off now. I knew at any moment they'd notice I wasn't with them. I hid behind one of the trees until they were out of sight, then headed west, creeping low, looking for a gate. Through the dried-up bracken, I glimpsed bars of rusted metal.

As I ran towards it, I heard shouting behind me. The thudding of boots.

I climbed over the gate and hopped down to the other side, stumbling as I kept on running, almost twisting my ankle. I didn't look back. I veered left as J.B. has directed, where I found the road. My chest tightened. My throat burned. I hadn't had a coughing fit in so long – now I could feel one coming on. I didn't dare stop. Pure adrenaline powered me on. That, and fear of what would happen to me if I was caught.

Eventually, I came to a small building with a mock Tudor façade, blue fairy lights strung up around the beams. Its sign had a picture of Lyfell Pike and the pub's name.

The Elixir.

Interference

I'D ALMOST FINISHED TRANSCRIBING our interviews and preparing a draft to share with Lucy. Then, yesterday, she emailed saying she didn't want to be involved in the project anymore, asking me to not share her story. No explanation why.

I've emailed back to ask if we could meet up and talk about it, at least, but she hasn't responded yet.

At first, I was angry. Now, I'm starting to worry. After pondering my conversation with Claire further, I wonder if I should have taken Lucy's concerns more seriously.

I'm sure it's all in my head, but I keep passing people in the street who resemble individuals Lucy described from the retreat. They all seem to be watching me.

I've started unplugging the phone at night.

Later the same day: Lucy was right all along. They have been stalking us – both of us. And with what's just happened, I'm beginning to understand the danger we're in.

I am so upset I can barely see my screen as I type this.

I took John Snow to the promenade for his constitutional. The weather was bad. There was a gale blowing, and I hadn't put my hearing aids in. Perhaps if I'd been wearing my hearing aids, I might have heard something besides the howling wind.

Sometimes John Snow bounds off ahead. Other times, he dawdles, sniffing every pebble we pass, and I have to whistle to get him to keep up. Today he wanted to savour everything, oblivious to the wind whipping my cheeks and making my eyes stream. When a particularly powerful gust almost blew my scarf off, I lost patience and ploughed on ahead without waiting for him to catch up.

I swear to you, I didn't see another soul on the promenade – I thought everyone else had made the sensible decision to stay inside. The only thing I noticed was the greyness of the sky and sea: a world drained of colour. Crows hopped across the beach and pecked the sand. Nothing unusual.

I'd walked a mile before I realised John Snow still hadn't caught up with me. I whistled and waited for him to run to my side. Whistled again. No sign of him. I retraced my steps along the promenade, calling his name. He knows he's not supposed to run onto the quicksand, but I leaned over the rail anyway, checking for paw prints. I even checked the train station in case he'd strayed onto one of the platforms. A woman was sat on a bench, waiting for a train. I asked her if she'd seen a beagle.

She told me yes – she'd seen two men with a beagle a few minutes ago and pointed me towards the station car park.

By the time I got there, the car park was empty.

'Where on earth have you been?' said Jen when I got home, drenched in rain and sweat. I'd been out for nearly four hours.

'The bastards took the dog.'

I broke down in tears. Regrettably, I wasted valuable time ranting about what I was going to do when I found them instead of immediately phoning the police.

I called them while Jen went out in her car to search for John Snow. She didn't seem to understand that he hadn't simply wandered astray, that he was miles away by now, in the back of a lunatic's van. Or worse.

I explained to the operator I'd been investigating a cult and they'd kidnapped my dog in retaliation. Jen came back; she hadn't found John Snow, of course. A couple of police officers came round and asked questions, took notes. Neither officer appeared to comprehend the urgency or danger of our situation. By this point, I was so exasperated, so distressed at the sight of John Snow's empty basket, I needed to excuse myself. When I returned, the living room door was closed. I heard one of the officer's voices behind it, asking, 'How long has this been going on for?' Jen replied: 'About two months.' The officer said, 'Is your husband receiving any medical attention?'

'So! You think I've gone insane,' I shot at Jen after the officers left.

She heaved a huge sigh. 'You want to know what I think? You've worked yourself up over your sister's letters. It's brought back very painful memories. And you're struggling to cope with all of it, which is understandable, but it's made you confused, Richard, and now you've accidentally lost the dog.'

I tried to explain this is exactly what Hartman and his people want her to think. They wanted to make me sound like the irrational, unreasonable one, and drive a wedge between my family and me.

'If they think I'm backing down, they've got another thing coming.'

I didn't like the look Jen gave me as I said this. I didn't like it at all.

End of Richard Blackley's manuscript

Afterword

The following letter from Olivia Blackley was enclosed with her father's manuscript.

1st May 2024

To whom it may concern,

Thank you for answering my emails and for your interest in my dad's manuscript. I must admit, I wasn't sure what kind of response I'd get, but after reading about the type of stuff you publish, strange stories and whatnot, it sounded like Dad's book could be a good fit. I'm determined to make his lifelong dream of becoming an author come true, even if he's not well enough to take charge of this himself anymore.

I discovered the manuscript while clearing out my parents' house. My mum died in October. There was a lot of stuff to sort through, and Dad wasn't able to help with any of it, of course. He has been living in a care home for a decade.

The manuscript was stowed away in a cupboard in the guest room, what used to be Dad's study. Mum never mentioned it to me. I think she didn't know what to do with it but couldn't bring herself to throw it away.

Dad's old computer was long gone by the time I found the manuscript, so I couldn't access his files to look for the electronic version. His manuscript mentions other interview transcripts, but the ones enclosed are the only ones I found. The sheets are exactly as I found them, in the same order, even tied with the same treasury tags.

You'll notice the manuscript ends abruptly, so I thought I'd give some context that might explain why.

On 30th January 2014, I'd just gone back to university after the winter break. I had lectures all morning. I was walking across campus to my next lecture when two strange men approached me. They asked if I knew Richard Blackley. I told them yes, I was his daughter. I thought maybe they were academics, friends of Dad's, although they didn't look like academics – they were dressed like Buddhist monks. Not exactly his crowd. They asked if I could go with them for a chat. I said I had to go to my lecture, and they said they'd wait for me outside. I told them I couldn't meet them after that because I had lectures all day. Honestly, I was just trying to get away from them, but I didn't want to seem rude. They suggested we could meet tomorrow instead, then let me go.

As soon as I got inside, I texted Dad, asking if he knew them. He rang me, but I couldn't speak, I was in a lecture. I had to put my phone on silent because he kept trying to call me.

When the lecture finished, I checked my phone, and I had loads of missed calls and voicemails. His voice sounded weird. He kept telling me to call him back and let him know I was okay.

When I called back, he answered on the second ring. He sounded relieved. He asked loads of questions about the two men, what they looked like, what they'd said. He asked me to stay put and wait for him to drive to campus and pick me up.

He was being ridiculous. I told him I was busy, I had classes, I couldn't just drop everything. He made me promise not to go anywhere on my own or speak to those men again, or to anyone else I didn't know.

I felt wary when I went back outside, keeping an eye out for those strange men. But I didn't see them again. I went on with my day, and the whole thing slipped my mind until that night, when Mum called me in tears.

I couldn't understand what she was saying. I had to keep asking her to repeat herself because the whole thing was so bizarre.

Dad had been arrested. Apparently, he'd driven to some wellness retreat in the Lake District and attacked two of their employees with a shovel, before someone managed to stop him. No one was seriously injured, thankfully, but they were pressing charges. They had it on CCTV.

Mum didn't know why he'd done it, but she knew he'd been writing a book about the retreat because he thought it had something to do with my Auntie Julie's death. I never met my auntie – she died when I was little. She committed suicide. I knew it had been a huge shock for the family and Dad had never gotten over it.

But that wasn't all. My dad was very unwell, Mum told me. She'd been to see him at the police station, and he wasn't himself at all. He kept babbling about saving us from Charles and Michael. Maybe they were the two men who'd approached me on campus. I mentioned this idea to Mum, but she didn't think it seemed likely, given how ill Dad seemed. She said it was a paranoid delusion of his.

Dad was diagnosed with VLOSLP (very late onset schizophrenia-like psychosis) and sectioned in February 2014. Shortly after, he was diagnosed with undifferentiated dementia. He is unable to communicate coherently. The criminal charges were dropped after he was acquitted on grounds of insanity at the Magistrates Court. Mum couldn't cope with Dad living at home, so he was moved into a facility that provides 24-hour care.

For years, I thought that was the whole story: that on 30th January 2014, my dad lost his mind. I never saw those two men again. I started to worry I'd only imagined them, and I was going mad, too, that I'd inherited Dad's illness. I went to the doctor for tests. I ended up having a nervous breakdown and dropped out from my course. It took me years to get my life back on track.

Then Mum died, and I found Dad's manuscript. To be honest, I don't know what to make of it – I can understand why Mum never mentioned it. I've not been able to track down this woman he interviewed. "Lucy". It's as if she never existed. Maybe she moved away, changed her name. I think he at least met someone at that support group because of all the detail in her story. But some things don't add up, like her escaping to that pub at the end – The Elixir closed down in 2006. We do know Dad was already showing signs of decline at the time he was writing the manuscript. It's possible he made the whole thing up.

I've checked out the retreat, too. It must have changed hands since Dad wrote about it – it's nothing like the place "Lucy" talked about, or where my auntie Julie went. There's plenty of information about it online, so many positive reviews and testimonials from people who've said it changed their lives. They've opened sister retreats across country. 'Places of healing in areas of natural beauty and tranquillity.' I'm thinking of going to one. The past few months since Mum died have been incredibly difficult, my migraines are worse than ever, and the medication I've been given is useless. Loads of reviewers say these retreats cured their chronic migraines.

While I don't know how much of Dad's manuscript is true, it makes me sad to think of his book going unread, since he obviously wanted to share this story with the world. I do hope it's something you'll consider publishing. If not, I'd be grateful if you could post it back to me via the return address on the envelope. This is the original copy.

Thank you for your time and consideration.

Sincerely,

Olivia Blackley

Acknowledgements

My deepest gratitude to:

My editor and publisher, Ariell Cacciola, for your passion right from the start for my idea for this story, as well as your expertise and support to help me bring it to fruition. I'm honoured to be published by Wild Hunt Books and to be part of the Northern Weird Project.

Luísa Dias for designing *The Retreat*'s incredibly beautiful cover.

My writing group, in particular Jae, Rosie, and Sarah, for your incisive feedback on excerpts of the manuscript at various stages of the drafting process. Your suggestions made the book better; your words of encouragement kept me going.

My dad, who tirelessly champions my writing and will now finally find out what this book's all about (sorry for all the secrecy).

My book club (and fellow femgore enthusiasts): Amy, Laura, and Sonja.

My friends and family, who've shown so much love for my debut book as well as excitement for this project.

Colleagues at Manchester Met for reading and supporting my writing.

Finally, to my partner, Dave, for always believing in me. I would not have written this book without you.

About the Author

Gemma Fairclough is a writer living in Manchester. She has a BA (Hons) in English Literature and a Master's in Contemporary Literature and Culture from the University of Manchester. She recently completed the Write Like a Grrrl programme and formed a writing group with peers from the course. A range of unsettling influences, including horror films, surrealist art, and folklore inspire her writing, which frequently centres upon experiences of alienation, grief, and aberrant desire. You can read a sample of her short fiction online: 'Please Make Sure You Take All Your Personal Belongings With You' (*Dear Damsels*), a story about an office worker with a fetish for automated female voices and 'Elemental' (*Mookychick*), a story about witchcraft and the power of belief.

Gemma's previous book *Bear Season* was published by Wild Hunt Books in 2024.

Twitter @GemFairclough
Instagram @gem.fairclough

About The Northern Weird Project

This book is a part of The Northern Weird Project
by Wild Hunt Books, a collection of six pocket-sized
novellas by authors who are writing and living in the
North of England.

Incorporating eerie and uncanny incidents, these
novellas investigate aspects of the North through setting, subject and character.

All books in this series are available to order from our
bookshop.
https://www.wildhuntbooks.co.uk/bookshop

More From The Northern Weird Project

This House Isn't Haunted But We Are
by Stephen Howard

Simon and Priya's young daughter has died in a tragic accident. Determined to heal their fracturing marriage, the couple move to the North Yorkshire Moors to renovate a dilapidated rural cottage. However, they just can't process their grief as increasingly eerie events unfold. A child's ghostly figure appears on the moors, doors lock themselves, and a mysterious stain grows from the loft. Is it their daughter haunting them or something else?

(Don't) Call Mum
by Matt Wesolowski

Leo is just trying to catch his train back home to the village of Malacstone in North East England. But there's disorder at the station, and when a loud young man heading for London boards the train accidentally, a usually easy journey descends into darkness and chaos. The train soon breaks down in the middle of nowhere, and as night falls, something...or someone steps out of the distance. Is it a man or something far more sinister?

The Off-Season
by Jodie Robins

It's the off-season in the seaside resort town of Blackpool, where Tommy never imagined he would return. His relationship has broken down, so he returns home to keep an eye on his widowed father. While counting down the hours before attending the funeral of a well-loved friend, a mysterious group turns up on the seafront. One by one, the locals are entranced by their presence until Tommy and his father can no longer resist the allure. Tommy soon discovers a secret desire his father has been harbouring for his entire life.

Good Boy
by Neil McRobert

After a boy vanishes on the outskirts of a small Northern town, a woman spies from her window a mysterious man digging a grave in the exact spot of the disappearance. However, when she confronts him, the man's true purpose is far more chilling than she could have imagined and the history of the town's fatal past unfolds. What has been hiding in this small northern town all these years? A gripping story of supernatural horror, nostalgia and mystery.

Turbine 34
by Katherine Clements

It's 2035 and England is experiencing the hottest summer in living memory. A 61-year-old environmental scientist is tasked with evaluating the impact of a controversial new wind farm on the West Yorkshire moors. Camped out alone at Turbine 34 which was built on the ancient peat bog, she soon discovers signs of the devastation caused by the construction, she begins to see things that shouldn't be there. She has dedicated her life to protecting the moor, but will it protect her?

Wild Hunt Books would like to thank the following Lifetime Supporters:

Daniel Sorabji
Jan Penovich
Blaise Cacciola

BECOME A SUPPORTER BY CONTACTING US AT
INFO@WILDHUNTBOOKS.CO.UK

The Publisher would also like to thank the following early supporters of The Northern Weird Project:

Aidan Smith
Alex Herod
Ali W
Alicia Lomas-Gross
Anthony Martin
Beth Baskett
Bethany Vare
Blair Rose
Carmen
Charlotte Platt
Charlotte Tierney
Emma Armshaw
Freya S
George Dunn
Heidi Marjamäki
Ianthe May
J. Aaron Courts CWO4, USMC, Retired
Jeff
Jennifer B. Lyday
K. Wicks
Kelsey Stoddard
Kirsty Logan
Laura Elliott
Lisa Elliott
Lynne G
Mandy Bublitz
Mark Taylor

Martyn Waites

Monica Voynovska

Nicola Leedham

Nina Woodcock

Rachel Bridgeman

Rosie Warfield

Samuel Best

Sheena E. Perez

Sonja Zimmermann

Sophy Holland

Stefanie Olivola

Stephanie Eleanor Henrichs Welch

Stewart Mack

Vince Fairclough

www.ingramcontent.com/pod-product-compliance
Ingram Content Group UK Ltd.
Pitfield, Milton Keynes, MK11 3LW, UK
UKHW041812220825

462162UK00001B/1